BLOOD BOND

SHIFTER PARANORMAL ROMANCE

ANN GIMPEL

Edited by

ANGELA KELLY

Illustrated by

FIONA JAYDE

CONTENTS

Blood Bond   v
Copyright Page   vii
Book Description, Blood Bond   ix

Chapter 1   1
Chapter 2   13
Chapter 3   25
Chapter 4   37
Chapter 5   49
Chapter 6   63
Chapter 7   75
Chapter 8   87
Chapter 9   101
Chapter 10   113
Chapter 11   127
Chapter 12   139
Chapter 13   151
Chapter 14   161
Epilogue   173

About the Author   183
Book Description: Highland Secrets, A Dragon Lore   185
Prequel
Highland Secrets, Chapter One   187

BLOOD BOND

UNDERGROUND HEAT, BOOK THREE

By
Ann Gimpel

Shifters keep their friends close and their enemies closer in a dark, gritty world where passion flares hot and sweet.

COPYRIGHT PAGE

Head of the shifter underground's security force, Johannes has his hands full. When Max, the underground's leader, is almost killed by sniper fire, Johannes breaks a cardinal rule to save his friend and makes a discovery about himself that changes everything.

Daria's been a healer in one capacity or another for hundreds of years, but wholesale slaughter aimed at wiping out her kin is something new. Called to the governor's mansion after Max gets shot, she finds him wallowing in a river of his own blood. By rights he should be dead. She questions Johannes, but he remains stubbornly silent—after telling her an outright lie.

If Johannes wasn't so knockout gorgeous, and she wasn't so wiped out, Daria would've left after treating Max. Instead, Johannes talks her into staying, then orders her to work for the underground. As head of security, it's his right to commandeer personnel. Daria is torn. Johannes is the most compelling man she's ever met, but he's also arrogant. Compounding the problem, her cat thinks he's their mate. After he runs roughshod over her, she doesn't care about anything except getting as far away from him as she can, but escape isn't possible.

A series of lethal attacks throw Daria into Johannes's path—and keep her there. He's desperately attracted to her, but anything beyond sex with any woman isn't part of his life plan. His cat says she's their mate, but it doesn't alter Johannes's staunch refusal to consider anything that might turn into love. He has his reasons. They've served him well, and he sees no reason to change them now.

CHAPTER 1

Johannes Takes wandered from the kitchen to the cozy study with its forbidden fireplace burning real, but equally forbidden, logs. Thank Christ for catalytic elements that all but obliterated any trace of smoke from the air outside. He eyed an overstuffed chair, but was too keyed up to sit, so he clasped his hands behind his back and watched the fire. The oblivion he sought eluded him, though.

Thoughts he usually kept tightly leashed pressed hard against his habitually imposed restraint. It was best when he kept his feelings buried, so they couldn't get in the way and trip him up. He moved closer to the fire, holding out his hands to its warmth. His people faced grave challenges. Trials that could mean the death of many, many shifters. Nothing less than his absolute attention to every single detail would do. There had to be a way through their current difficulties, but he was damned if he saw a clear road.

Beyond the threat of genocide for his kin, personal demons badgered him.

While he was delighted Max Sigayev and Audrey Westen were mated—and it had been an honor to be the one joining them—still their joy underscored his loneliness. He and Max went back close to two hundred years. They'd met in a very different time, a time when finding clean air and water wasn't a problem. A time when shifters were valued and could walk free with their heads high.

Not anymore.

Thanks to a U.S. government edict, copied by every other industrialized nation, shifters had become persona non grata. Reviled. Shunned. Rounded up and killed.

Johannes curled his hands into fists so hard his nails cut into his palms. Maybe because he'd been around for virtually all of Max's life, the other shifter hadn't ever asked him very many questions about himself. Johannes's vague replies about working in espionage had been accurate enough—and they'd satisfied Max's curiosity.

What he'd left out was that his original employer had been Odysseus.

Johannes was the first shifter, created by Ceres, guardian of the earth, and he was immortal. A corner of his mouth twisted downward. He'd been an experiment. The goddess kept the shifter part, but decided the earth would quickly become overpopulated if none of them ever died, so subsequent shifters weren't dealt the immortal card.

He'd faded in and out of sight over his better than two thousand years of existence. Shifters were long lived, but nothing like him. In truth, his relationship with Max and the shifter underground were the closest he'd come to permanence in a very long time. Ceres had made it abundantly clear he wasn't to tell anyone about the extra gift she'd given him.

And he never had.

Johannes sank into a squat before the flames and shook his head. Gift, his ass. More like a curse. Since he couldn't tell anyone, it had limited his congress with women to sex. Lots of it with a variety of intriguing partners, but he'd always run like hell if he started to care. Even absent finding his mated one—which hadn't happened— he'd been afraid to fall in love, knowing he'd have to watch the woman die, and then the next one, and the next.

"Oh for Christ fucking sake," he muttered and pushed to his feet. Looking back never did any good, never yielded different answers. Just the same old, tired details.

Maybe a walk in the moonlight would help. He pushed open a side door and engaged his mountain cat senses, sniffing. Max and Audrey had been out here—and not very long ago—but they were back inside. He grabbed a jacket off a hook and slipped into it to cut the chill of the winter night.

The old mansion he and Max had purchased sat in one of Sacramento's older neighborhoods on a generous piece of land. They'd bought it years before—just like they'd bought real estate all around the globe to assure they had choices, in case they couldn't remain in a particular location. The place had remained empty until Max came up with his harebrained scheme to run for California governor. Max was so certain he'd win, he'd begun shipping things from one of their many European manor houses to furnish this one months before the election.

"Harebrained, but brave," Johannes's mountain cat commented from his permanent spot in Johannes's mind.

"Can't fault him for lacking guts." Johannes grinned, but his smile faded fast. *"Haven't heard much from you lately. Do you have any ideas for how we play out the endgame?"*

"You called a spade a spade," the cat said quietly. *"Whatever happens over the next few weeks will determine the outcome of the war humans are waging against us."*

"You didn't exactly answer me." Johannes made his way to a good-sized pond and watched ripples in the water from koi that swam in its depths.

"Too many variables. Since we have no idea what the opposition will do next, it makes it hard to plan. We also don't know if all the shifter splinter groups will join our effort."

Bending, Johannes selected a flat rock and skipped it over the pond's surface. The sad truth was not all the rogue shifters would join the underground, and those that didn't would end up cannon fodder—murdered by one side or the other. He'd seen that particular scenario play itself out many times.

It made him sad—and angry—but there wasn't much he could do to alter it. The sound of one of the house doors snicking open caught at his sensitive feline hearing. Who the hell could it be? Surely not Max and Audrey, who were likely locked in one more heated embrace.

He rolled his eyes and trotted toward the far side of the house where he'd heard the door open. Shifters loved sex—lived for it—and mated sex was the best there was, yielding an inexhaustible well of passion. Another of Ceres's gifts, she'd substituted pleasure for immortality.

Audrey's mother, Bethea Westen, walked a few paces from the house. When she saw him, she came to a halt. "Sorry. Guess I wasn't the only one who couldn't sleep."

She met his gaze with hazel eyes a lot like Audrey's. Bethea looked like a slightly older version of her daughter, with curly strawberry-blonde hair and a tall, curvaceous figure. Tonight she was wrapped in a black, wool coat that almost scraped the ground.

"You're worried about emerging from hiding." Johannes stated it as fact because he was practically certain it was true.

Bethea nodded. "Of course. Who wouldn't be?" She hesitated. "It's more than that, though. Ron thinks there will be fighting. Lots of it." Tears sheened her eyes, but she didn't brush them aside. "I know most of you shifters don't take me seriously because I'm only a human, but I love Ron. I don't think I could stand it if anything happened to him, and me telling him to leave the rough stuff for the younger ones gets me nowhere. As shifters go, he is young."

Johannes wasn't certain what to say. He didn't want to lie. Besides, she wouldn't believe him anyway, so he maintained a supportive silence.

"Sorry. I didn't mean to say that much. It just sort of slipped out." Bethea turned to go.

"The yard is big enough for us both," Johannes said. "Don't let me chase you back inside."

She eyed him. "Where are you from?"

"Why would you ask?"

A sheepish smile curved her lips. "Guess it wasn't very polite of me, but I was trying to figure it out over dinner. Sometimes you sound German. Sometimes Austrian. There were even a few times when you had a hint of a Russian accent like Max, though his speech is pretty purely American most of the time."

"I've lived a long time in a lot of different places," he murmured.

"Yes, but where were you from originally?" she persisted. "Unless you don't want to tell me, which is all right too."

He smiled back. What could the harm be? "Greece," he said. "I was born in Greece."

"Really?" She sharpened her gaze, and her intensity reminded him a lot of Audrey. "I never would've guessed."

"You'd be in good company. Not many do."

"You're part of the underground's security force, aren't you?"

He quested for a noncommittal response. "You might say that."

"So you're a good one to ask. What do you think will happen with Ron and the others emerging from hiding and joining up with the underground?"

Seems like the question of the hour tonight.

"I wish I had a solid answer for you, but there are too many unknowns. Once we see how many shifters we have to work with, we'll be able to determine what kind of offensive strategy might work." He paused for a beat. "The other alternative—but it's much weaker to my way of thinking—is to defend ourselves against whatever they throw our way."

Bethea furrowed her forehead, clearly considering his words. "But won't you do that anyway? Defend yourselves from attack, I mean?"

"Of course. I didn't explain myself very well. The best campaigns are a combination of offense and defense."

Her next words came slowly. "I guess no one would be exempt. No shifters, anyway."

"The more who join the cause, the more likely we'll prevail." Johannes forged ahead before she could say more. "I can't believe you like the way you've lived these past two years. Skulking about. Living on throwaways and whatever else you could scrounge. It's no way to craft a life."

"Ron and the others were sure this would all blow over—at the beginning."

"Except it just got worse. We didn't form the underground immediately. Only after they started rounding us up and throwing us in prison."

"I guess that's what happens when you give in to bullies." Her voice was soft. "It encourages them to do even worse to you."

"You're right." Johannes had balled his hands into fists, and he flexed his fingers to relax the tension thrumming through his body. "I tell you this, madam. We will win this. Shifters deserve to survive. We hold magic that has the power to enrich everyone's lives. Earth would be a grim place without us."

He stopped shy of launching into the myth about Ceres searching for her daughter and how it spawned the cold, bitter seasons. Even though gods and goddesses were long absent from view, he had no doubt they still existed. What would Ceres do if shifters—her creation—were wiped out?

He had a feeling her retribution would be swift and brutal. And since he was the only one who couldn't die, he'd at least get to witness it.

"Madam, huh?" Bethea's voice broke into his thoughts. "Your Old Country roots are showing. I have a feeling there're things you're not saying—"

The side door Bethea had used swung open, and Ron loped to his wife's side. "There you are. What are you doing outside bothering Johannes?"

"She's not bothering me," Johannes said. "We were having an interesting philosophical discussion."

Ron snorted. "Yeah. I'll bet. She was probably out here trying to figure out a way to talk you into making certain I end up with a desk job in whatever crapola the humans throw our way next."

"No, she actually wasn't. She is worried, but it's only because she loves you." Johannes blew out a breath. "I'm going back inside. If the two of you want to walk through the grounds, they're quite safe."

Without waiting for them to answer, he slipped past and strode around the mansion to the door into the study. The fire was burning low, but he didn't feed it. Time to turn in. He didn't sleep much, but maybe if he rested his eyes and body he'd come up with a better plan to deal with the shit storm heading their way.

Humans had good intel, and they had to know about the influx of shifters swelling the underground's ranks. He picked up a bottle of Madeira and a snifter and walked slowly upstairs. Max lived in a suite at one end of the third floor. Johannes occupied the entirety of the fourth.

In front of the door leading to his rooms, he tipped his chin so the retinal scanner could read him. The locking mechanism ticked open, and he walked into the large, open space he'd crafted to please his aesthetic needs—and those of his cat. Because his living space took up the entire floor, every wall was lined with windows.

Johannes liked it that way. Both the sunrise and sunset glittered through leaded glass panes. At the moment, they framed an almost full moon. A large bed butted into one corner. An even larger desk littered with myriad computer gadgetry sat across from it. Above the electronics, a wall-sized screen blinked with messages and intelligence gathered from around the world by Johannes's many connections. Bookshelves ran from the bottom of the windows to the floor, overflowing with books and scrolls. A veritable fortune in antiquarian books graced his shelves, and he used many of them as ongoing resource materials. Nothing even remotely akin to them were available through the vid feed. Libraries had thinned out years before. No one had the funds to maintain very many of them.

He kicked off his shoes and removed the jacket he'd plucked from downstairs. It actually belonged to Max, so he should return it, but he'd do that tomorrow. Not much remained of the night as it was. He pulled his sweater over his head, draped it over a chair, and unfastened his trousers. In between getting undressed, he poured himself half a snifter of the Madeira and sipped, savoring its exotic, spicy scent.

Once he was nude, he wrapped himself in a robe and padded into the bathroom at the far end of his suite. Open like the rest of the space, it hosted a highly illegal deep soaking tub made of creamy, red-veined marble. The government had outlawed tubs years ago since they wasted water. Johannes controlled data flowing into and out of the mansion, so masking water use was easy enough to finesse. Not that he was into wasting resources, but he did enjoy the occasional soak. The floor was rare, ivory-toned slate imported from Ceylon. In truth, it was more of an indulgence than the tub.

He killed the Madeira and thought about a bath. In the end, he settled for a shower, letting the body jets from the wall mounted unit pummel him as he soaped and rinsed. The water had a stimulating effect—not quite what he was hoping for—and his penis swelled.

Johannes shut the shower off and grabbed a fluffy dark brown towel. Everything had a *stimulating* effect since Max and Audrey's lust made the house smell like an upscale bordello to his sensitive nose. His cock twitched to full attention, curved against his belly. He tried to ignore it, but sensation coursed through him, along with a visual of the last woman he'd fucked.

Finding partners was easy. Shifters held an easy grace, and humans were desperately attracted to them. All he had to do was wander into any bar or shop or restaurant, and women practically threw themselves at him. Sometimes, if they smelled appealing to him and his cat agreed, he took them up on their offered delights.

Curving a hand around his ridged flesh, he gave in to desire heating his blood. A woman was better than his hand, but right now he wanted expediency, and he wouldn't be clear-headed until after he came.

He moved from the bathroom to a thick Oriental carpet covering hardwood flooring and sat down, resting his back against the end of his bed. A flick of his wrist brought the wall screen to life. A few more adjustments, and one of his favorite fantasies flared to life.

A stunning Asian with long, straight dark hair that kissed her hips waltzed straight toward him and stopped, legs slightly spread. Small, conical breasts with peaked nipples teased him. He'd built the simulation, so it met his sexual needs perfectly.

"Johannes." The woman ran her tongue over full lips, and her dark eyes glittered with lust. "I've missed you." She stroked her hands down the clean lines of her body and shoved her hair aside, baring everything for him.

He decided which of several voice-activated programs he wanted and asked, "What have you missed?"

In this simulation, it would be just her. Others included more women and even another man or two.

"This." She closed a hand over one breast, tweaking and twirling her nipple. "And this." She dipped her other hand between her legs, tilting her pelvis, so he could watch her masturbate.

As she teased her breasts, and rubbed her clit in hard, little circles, he tightened his hold around his cock, adding some saliva to lubricate things. Asian girl moaned, and her skin developed a rosy hue as her excitement mounted. Johannes pinched his nipples to heighten his sensation and jacked himself hard. He and Asian girl had done this enough, he could time his climax to almost exactly match hers.

"Tell me." His voice was taut with lust.

"I know. Tell you when I'm almost there." She shut her eyes and rubbed herself harder. In a single, fluid motion she bent to one side and picked up a dildo.

Even though he knew what would happen next, he never tired of watching her stretch full length on a plush futon and slide the fake cock inside her. She positioned her legs so he could watch her fuck herself, and when she pulled the dildo out, it glistened with her secretions. One hand manipulated the sex toy; the other traded between her breasts and her clit.

"Yes, Johannes. Close." She looked right at him because that was how he'd programmed it. Her nipples were hard buds, and her golden skin glowed with desire.

He tweaked his nipples again and jacked himself harder, faster. His balls tightened, and he reached behind them, pressing the spot that always made him wild with lust.

Asian girl was panting, gasping for air. Her eyes flicked open. "Now," she shouted. "Come now."

Almost as if the hologram had power, semen bubbled from his balls and shot from his cock in sheets of delight. His hips pumped and writhed, and he sucked air, maximizing every shred of pleasure as his cock juddered in his hand.

"That was wonderful. Let's do it again soon." Asian girl winked lazily, and the screen shaded to blackness.

"You've turned that into an art form," his cat noted wryly. *"How about finding us a shifter to fuck?"*

Johannes struggled to normalize his breathing. Guilt smote him. Holograms added spice to his non-existent love life, but they did less than nothing for his cat. Sure, it came whenever he did, but it knew the simulation—and stimulation—wasn't real.

Hell, he knew it wasn't real too, but it was better than nothing, and it hadn't taken him much time to build the various programs he used to jack off with.

I'm making excuses.

"Sorry," he told his cat. *"Maybe with all the shifters coming out of hiding, our mate will show up."*

"You know that's not true." His cat's voice held a different note, one Johannes hadn't heard before.

"What do you mean?"

"There's no mated one for us. We're the only immortal shifter bondmates in the entire universe."

The cat's sadness reverberated inside Johannes, but he tried to soothe his bond animal. *"Just because there might not be a mated one for us is no reason we can't enjoy sex with a shifter."*

"We can. And we have. But what's the point? I appreciate you trying to make me feel better, but I'm done talking for now. I withdraw my request for you to find us a shifter for sex."

Johannes got to his feet, grabbed a towel, and cleaned up his mess. As usual, his cat cut to the heart of things. They might find a shifter to have sex with—or even fall in love—but the magic of the mate bond would always elude them. If it hadn't knocked on their door in better than two thousand years, it never would.

"Enough." He spoke aloud to force himself to move forward.

A quick glance at his mostly unopened messages convinced him they could wait. Too many to deal with, and he was tired. Closing eyes for half an hour would help his concentration. He threw himself face down on the bed and was asleep almost before his head hit the pillow.

Frantic pounding on his door dragged him awake. A gray dawn flickered through the windows as he thrust the muzziness of sleep aside. He'd obviously done more than nap. The pounding escalated.

What the fuck?

Claws poked through his fingers, but he held his cat back. *"Not yet. We don't know what's wrong."*

ohannes stumbled to the door and pulled it open. If he'd been thinking, he'd have sent magic through it to see who was out there, but he didn't. In truth, there were very few choices. Bad guys didn't knock. Max knew how to get in, so that left Audrey or her parents.

Audrey almost fell into the room. Her eyes were wounded, glazed with shock. She grabbed his arm, smearing him with blood. The air thickened with the metallic scent of it. "You have to come right now."

"Did something happen to Max? Tell me."

"Yes. Max. He was— We were— Shit!" She pounded her fist into a wall and yelped. "Out on our balcony. We were outside to welcome the new day, and someone shot him." Her face crumpled. "You have to come. He's still alive, but there's so much blood I don't understand why he's still breathing. Can we call 911? Would a hospital know what to do? I'd have called them already, but I wasn't sure if it was a safe place for shifters." Sobs ripped from her.

He realized he was still naked and slithered into a pair of jeans. A fine edge of suspicion intruded. There hadn't been any attempts on

Max's life before Audrey took the serum to turn her from a human with shifter blood into someone who could actually shift.

"I could give a fuck less about you being naked. Hurry," she shrieked.

Johannes flew down the stairs with her hard on his heels. "Audrey," he shot over his shoulder. "Don't lose it. I need your help. Call this number." He rattled off a series of digits. "Tell them Code Four."

"Who are they? What will they do?" Her voice shrilled with hysteria.

"We have our own doctors. Just do it."

He heard the clicks as she fed the number into her wrist computer and her voice requesting help and giving their location.

Good. At least that part's done.

He burst into Max's suite. Audrey had dragged him inside, and he lay in a widening pool of blood. Johannes launched himself to the floor next to Max and began a quick exam.

"What can I do?" Audrey stood over them.

"While I figure out what I can fix, tell me exactly what happened. Don't titrate it. Don't leave anything out."

"Not much to tell. We got up at five, and Max thought it would be nice to watch the sunrise, so we dressed and went out onto the balcony. We hadn't been there five minutes when I heard a hovercraft flying really low—well below minimums."

She took a shuddering breath and went on. "Max looked up and said, 'Bastards. I'm calling that one in. It can't be fifty feet above the ground.'"

Breath whistled through Audrey's teeth like a steam engine gone awry. "Max twisted his body to peer at his wrist computer, and I heard the bullet. Shit! If he hadn't moved, it would've gone right through his head."

A low, keening moan escaped her, and she clapped a hand over her mouth. "Sorry."

Johannes couldn't take his attention away from Max to comfort her. He applied pressure to the wound just below Max's shoulder. He hadn't found an exit wound, which meant the bullet was still lodged in his body. Probably one of the older-style hollow points that did maximum damage once they were inside a body. Judging from the amount of blood, the shell had clipped a major vessel.

"Talk to me," Audrey pleaded. "I'm holding on by a thread here. Can you save him? Who's on their way here? Are you sure we shouldn't call 911?"

"Maybe I can save him. No on the 911 call. Worst part is how much blood he's lost," Johannes said, addressing some of her questions.

Harsh pounding on the door of Max's suite sent Audrey running for it. Out of the corner of his eyes, Johannes saw her parents crowd inside and heard the desperate note in their voices as Audrey filled them in.

"Goddammit." He sent his mind voice straight to Max—and his wolf. *"Hang on. Help's on the way."*

But the only sign Max was still alive were shallow, bubbling breaths. Johannes pressed harder on the wound, but blood continued to leak in a steady stream.

"You have to," his cat piped up. *"No choice."*

Even though his bond animal's reference was oblique, Johannes understood completely. Max was dying. His life energy ebbed by the moment. Soon it would flicker out entirely. No time to wait for the shifter docs.

No time for anything but a last ditch effort.

He allowed one hand to shift to a paw. That done, he extended a razor sharp claw from its sheath and cut a narrow line through one of his veins. Once blood flowed, he removed the piece of clothing he'd used for a pressure bandage away from Max's wound and allowed his own blood to flow into the other shifter. Maybe, just maybe, a touch of immortality would make the difference.

It was the only tool he had left to use.

"What are you doing?" Ron Westen had crossed the room and stood over them. "Shouldn't we have called in our own docs?"

"I did, Daddy," Audrey said. "They're not here yet."

"What does it look like I'm doing?" Johannes snarled, using anger to cover his actions. "I'm trying to save his life."

"Sorry," Ron muttered. "I was only trying to help."

"Yeah." Johannes softened his tone. "I know. I'm sorry too. Could one of you go downstairs and let the medics in once they arrive. Wouldn't hurt to call back to get an ETA."

"I'm on it." Audrey tapped her wrist computer with determined fury as if she could pound better answers out of it.

"How much blood?" he asked his cat.

"Maybe another minute or two. It's not like— Wait. His wolf is trying to talk with me."

Johannes watched Max with a critical eye. It seemed the gray pallor was shading to a slightly warmer shade. He made a decision and focused magic to close the cut in his arm. Replacing the blood-soaked clothing over Max's wound and pressing hard, he took the other man's hand and exhorted him to live, goddammit.

But there was no answering pressure against his fingers.

"What's going on?" he asked his cat, too impatient to wait for his animal to spew whatever it knew.

"Max's wolf thinks they'll make it. He wants to know what's in your blood. Sensed it was different from other shifter serum."

"What'd you tell him?" He kept his question casual. Now wasn't the time to get into a fight—with anyone. He had his hands full holding Max on this side of the veil.

"I'm surprised you'd even ask. I said he was mistaken. When he said he wasn't, I insisted it was likely a result of coming so close to death. If Max dies in human form—"

"Spare me. His wolf will be lost wandering in the in-between and won't ever be able to form another pair bond."

Noise from downstairs snagged his attention. Had to be the medics.

"It's about fucking time," he muttered, wondering what the hell had taken them so long. Supposedly, they kept hovercraft ready to go at a moment's notice.

"In here," Audrey's voice rang. "Hurry."

Johannes glanced up to see a medium height woman with hair so black it looked like a deep, rich blue, drawn back from her face in a severe bun. She would've been striking with tip-tilted, dark Asian eyes, if she hadn't looked so haggard. Blood-stained pale green scrubs hugged her body, and when he looked closer, he noticed blood streaked down one of her cheeks. She was slender, with just a hint of breasts beneath her medical garb and slightly flared hips.

"I'd get up," he said, his voice curt, "but I can't. You look like you came from a war zone."

"I did." The woman turned and yelled, "Barney, get that bag up here. Now."

"Is he the doctor?" Johannes asked.

She curled her lip derisively. "No, macho asshole. I am. He's my nurse." She loped across the room, settled on Max's other side, and busied herself examining him. Closing her teeth over her lower lip, she frowned.

"What?" Johannes asked.

She pushed his hands away. "I can take over from here. Judging from where the bullet entered and how much blood he's lost, this man should be dead. I don't understand why he isn't."

Another man, presumably Barney, sprinted into the room and dropped an overflowing medical bag next to the doc. "Here. Sorry. I had to repack it from shit in the hovercraft since we used so much—"

"Shut up and hold a light for me. So long as the patient is unconscious, I'm going to try to go after that bullet. Then I can sew him up, once and for all."

Barney dug for what she requested, and the two of them bent over Max's inert form. Judging from their ability to function with a minimum of communication, they'd worked together for a while.

The nurse was tall, thin to the point of gauntness, with a shock of bright red hair that fell into his dark eyes. His scrubs looked even scruffier than the doc's.

Johannes rocked back on his heels. His hands were coated with Max's blood, mixed with his own, and his jeans were splattered with it. He cast a surreptitious glance at his forearm, grateful to see his wound was well on the way to being healed. At least for now, his secret was still safe. The doctor, with her eagle eyes, probably didn't miss a whole hell of a lot. Not that his intervention was something she'd even begin to guess at in her wildest imaginings.

"Might be a bit tardy with the introductions, but I'm Johannes—" he began.

"Yeah, and this is Max Sigayev. I'd have to have been sequestered on another planet not to recognize him." The doctor arranged clamps around Max's wound and sprayed something in it that stopped the outflow of blood. She waved an instrument with a lighted display over Max's shoulder, and a grim smile formed on her stark features. "Son of a bitch. Looks like we got a break."

Barney handed her an instrument, and seconds later, she'd extracted the shell.

Johannes bent close. "Is it intact?"

The doctor nodded. "Yeah. Not one of those exploding motherfuckers. Thank Christ!"

"Can I sit next to him and hold one of his hands?" Audrey asked.

The doctor's head snapped up and her nose twitched. "Who are you? Never mind. You're his mate. Yeah. Just don't get in my way."

"Do you have a name?" Johannes asked. Manners clearly weren't high on the doctor's hit parade.

"Doesn't everyone?"

"Are you going to tell me what it is?" Irritation sluiced through him. "I'm the head of the underground's security force, and—"

"Daria Sata. I'd move so you could get a closer look at my creds, but I'm a little busy here."

"Can you tell me anything about the war zone you came from?"

Johannes added the tiniest bit of compulsion to his request. He needed to know what had turned to shit in the few hours he'd slept.

Daria trained her dark gaze on him, eyes flashing with irritation. "Let me concentrate on what I'm doing. I'm tired, and I don't want to make a mistake. Then you can talk with me."

"Fair enough."

Johannes got to his feet. Ron and Bethea were huddled next to the door, looking worried. "Max is going to make it," he said. "I'm headed upstairs to shower and get dressed. How about if the two of you get something happening for breakfast? Normally, I cook, but things would go faster if—"

"Of course." Bethea laid a hand on his arm. "I'm grateful to have something to do. I'll get coffee on for all of us too."

"Don't make anything for us," Barney said. "We can't stay."

"Of course you can," Ron cut in. "Everyone needs to eat." He and his wife disappeared down the stairs.

Johannes turned the other way and climbed to the fourth floor. *"Did you talk further with Max's wolf?"*

"No. He's just relieved his bondmate will survive."

That makes two of us, Johannes thought sourly.

He'd been certain Max was done for in the first few moments after he settled by the other shifter's side. Life energy held a particular feel when it was about to be snuffed out. If he'd arrived five minutes later, Max would've been gone.

"Do you think Audrey is mixed up in this?" he asked his cat. The animal's instincts were frequently more astute than his own.

"Why do you think she might be?" The cat's response was cagy. Responding to a question with another was one of its stalling techniques when it wasn't certain of something.

Johannes walked through his open door and pushed his jeans down his hips. His next stop was the shower to get the stink of blood off his skin.

"It's all circumstantial," he said as he washed himself. *"The other two attempts on Max's life happened after Audrey took the serum—"*

"No," his cat cut in. *"Only the second one. Her debut shift happened later in the evening—after the first attempt in the elevator."*

"And you know this how?" Johannes dried himself off and went in search of clean clothes for the day. He opted for casual, with dark slacks and a cream-colored long-sleeved shirt, topped by a pale blue cashmere sweater. Socks and loafers followed.

"How else? I spoke with her wolf."

Johannes grinned in spite of himself. The bond animals all knew one another. *"It sounds like you're friends with her bond animal."*

"Indeed I am, and I trust her. She waited a long time for Audrey to find a way through."

Johannes ran a comb through his damp, dark brown locks. His hair was long enough to bind into a queue, but today he left it loose. Stubble lined his jaw, but he didn't bother to shave.

"So you're not worried Audrey might be behind these attempts on Max's life." There. Better to get things out in the open. His cat didn't respond well to subtlety.

"How could she be? You heard her. It was his idea to go outside this morning."

"Did you check to make certain she was telling the truth? Because I didn't."

"I don't have to check. I just know these things." A rustling snarl moved through his mind. *"After all the time we've spent together—"*

Johannes made a chopping motion with one hand. *"Enough. It's been a hell of a morning, and the day's barely begun."*

He checked in with his electronic intel and groaned. One of the splinter groups had stormed an underground safe house in the South Bay. Apparently, not all of the rogue shifters were going to get with the program and join forces with the underground.

"Shit!" He pounded a fist down on his crowded desk. Battles you fought on more than one front were difficult, fraught with the unknown. A phrase ran through his head.

The enemy of my enemy is my friend.

But what if you couldn't tell whose side someone was on? What then? It made it damned difficult to fight next to someone who was just as likely to turn on you and slit your throat, as they were to be your ally.

"You think too much," his cat noted snidely.

"That's a good trait." Johannes answered out loud. The cat could hear either way.

"Not always." A pause. *"The doctor is another mountain cat."*

"So?" Johannes tapped keys, crafting a response to today's attack that would go out on the underground's shielded vid feed.

"She doesn't have a mate."

"So what? She's about as warm as a rattlesnake. Besides, I thought you'd given up on finding live bait for us to seduce." He was still focused on a strategy to counteract the fuckers who'd blown one of their safe houses to Hell.

Rather than answering, his cat subsided into silence. Johannes knew him well enough to understand he wasn't done, but that he'd given up—for now.

Audrey blew through his open door, her face wreathed in a relieved smile. "Max is awake, and he's asking for you. And for coffee." Laughter bubbled from her throat. "If he wants his cuppa joe, I know he's going to be just fine." She raced back downstairs, her heels clattering down the risers.

Johannes shut down his vid feed and followed her.

Max was propped on cushions against one wall, blond hair splayed down his shoulders. His color wasn't great, but his ice-blue eyes were open and he extended a hand. "Thank you, old friend. You saved my life."

Daria sat next to Max, stethoscope pressed to his chest. She looped the instrument around her neck and stared at Johannes. "What exactly did you do?" Her dark eyes bored into him. "I'd like to know. The bullet clipped a vein and he basically bled out."

"Watch it," his cat cautioned. *"She holds our magic and knows when someone's not telling the truth."*

Johannes made his way to Max's side. Squatting, he grasped

Max's hand but focused his words at Daria. "It was nothing. Mostly I kept more blood from pumping out while we waited for you and your nurse to show up."

Daria frowned and opened her mouth.

Before she could ask an uncomfortable question, Johannes said, "What do you remember about the attack, Max? It's really important, or I wouldn't ask."

Max drew his blond brows together. "It was odd. I'd just herded Audrey onto the balcony, so we could watch the sunrise. It seemed like a romantic way to start the day. Then this damned hovercraft buzzed us, and someone shot me."

"Someone from inside the craft?"

Max nodded. "It would nearly have to be. Only one shot, though." He smiled wryly. "If I were the assassin, I'd have pumped more than one bullet into my target."

"Let's be grateful for small favors," Johannes muttered.

"Indeed," Daria seconded.

Max shook his head. "I'd bet my last bundle of black market cash that the craft was hanging around, hoping for a shot at me. Damned creepy. Wonder how many days they've staked out my house."

"None. I'd have detected them," Johannes said stiffly, cut to the quick by Max's inference something could've escaped his notice for very long.

"Aw, shit." Max rolled his eyes. "I'm not thinking. Didn't mean to infer you're not competent."

Ron walked into the room. "Bethea sent me to let you know soup's on." He glanced at Max. "If you feel up to it, I can help you downstairs."

"Of course I feel up to it," Max blustered, but without much of his usual bravado.

"Is it okay?" Ron addressed his question to Daria.

After a measured pause, she nodded. "His shifter physiology gives him an edge. Now that the bullet is gone, and he has enough blood in his body to sustain life, he'll heal fast."

Johannes pushed upright. Between him and Audrey and Ron, they levered Max upright. "Grab me some fresh clothes," he said to Audrey. "I can change downstairs so I don't destroy breakfast for everyone by smelling like my own blood."

"Sure." She rifled through drawers, and then she and her father helped Max walk down the stairs.

Barney chucked blood-soaked bandages into a polybag. "Ready to roll, boss?" he asked Daria.

She nodded, but looked so exhausted the skin beneath her eyes was gray.

"Please stay for breakfast," Johannes murmured. "I got the intel I need about last night's disaster off the vid feed, so I promise I won't pester you with questions."

"I shouldn't."

Barney, who'd looked hopeful, turned away and continued packing up.

"You have to eat sometime," Johannes pressed. "When's the last time you either ate or slept?"

Daria ran a hand down her face, distorting her features and then grimaced. "Fuck. Shouldn't touch my face. Haven't washed my hands. A long time. Maybe two days."

"All the more reason." Johannes aimed for kindness, not something that came easily for him. *Kind* was for suckers. *Kind* got you killed.

She swayed on her feet, and Barney reached out a hand to steady her.

"Okay," she said. "Coffee and breakfast might go well right about now." She slitted her eyes at Johannes. "I haven't forgotten you never answered me about exactly what you did to save Max. I really want to know."

Johannes locked gazes with her. "Maybe you can tell me about yourself too."

She snorted. "Quid pro quo, huh? Maybe so."

CHAPTER 3

$\mathcal{D}$aria got to her feet and rotated her shoulder blades. She was past tired. It reminded her of her modern medical training when she'd been on call every other night, sometimes for months. Tired M.D.s made mistakes, most of which got swept under the rug by other M.D.s. Her shifter senses provided an edge, but even they felt dull right now.

"See you downstairs, Sata. Thanks for relenting about breakfast." Barney shouldered their medical bag and started down the stairs after Johannes.

Before she left, Daria took a few breaths to center herself. Johannes was one good-looking man. Tall and broad shouldered, with eyes the color of cut emeralds. His dark brown hair had golden streaks in it, and the way he held himself exuded a raw sensuality that had her cat so spun out, all it had done since she walked into the room was broadcast a litany of what they could do with him— once they got him alone and naked.

Daria sucked in a tight breath. She couldn't remember the last time she'd had a day off. Or a night to herself. Let alone the indulgence of sex with anyone. Shifters were under siege, so she'd worked unstintingly, feeling it was the least she could do. She was old, and she'd practiced medicine under one guise or another since the fourteen hundreds. Of course back then, she'd been the local goodwife or wise woman or midwife.

When clerics weren't trying to hang her out to dry for witchcraft.

She stifled a grin. Even though shifters were in everyone's gunsights now, times hadn't changed all that much. There'd always been an underdog, and sometimes it was shifters.

It was the way of the world.

The smells of breakfast wafted up the stairwell, reminding her she was starving, so she hurried down lushly carpeted stairs, following her nose to locate the dining room. Along the way, she ducked into a lavish, slate bathroom to wash her hands and face. The reflection of her bloodstained scrubs in the mirror drew her face into a scowl. She had clean duds in the hovercraft. She ought to swap out her soiled clothing, but didn't want to take the time. She could change after she and Barney left.

Apparently Max had done well for himself, judging from his house and furnishings. She'd never cared much for things. Consequently, her home was the top floor of a remodeled brownstone in San Francisco. It contained a comfortable bed, state-of-the-art computer equipment, and a few things she couldn't bear to part with, collected over the long years of her life. Not that she spent much time there to appreciate them.

Everyone was already seated around a long, polished table when she walked into the dining room. Johannes got to his feet and offered her a smile that made her heart flutter oddly. "There you are. I was getting ready to hunt you down."

"Watch it." She smiled back. "My cat might take you up on that. She loves a good game of chase."

"Funny, so does mine." He gestured to an antique sideboard. "Help yourself."

"Thanks, I will. And it's not funny at all. It's the nature of cats." She plucked a plate from a stack at the end of the sideboard and loaded it with a selection of eggs, ham, sausage, and fresh fruit. Setting her plate down in an empty spot at the table, she poured herself a cup of fragrant, dark coffee.

"I haven't seen this much non-processed food in quite a while, but I won't make anyone uncomfortable by asking how you came by it."

"Appreciated." Max, who was looking much better, inclined his head. "Our safe houses are well stocked, and we operate our own farms."

"Yes, but I don't live in one of your safe houses. In the rare moments when I'm not working, I'm stuck with ration coupons like everyone else."

Before she sat down, she walked to Max's side and lifted his shirt to check his wound for redness or swelling. "Already healing nicely," she pronounced.

Max's mate sat next to him, and she patted his hand possessively. "Thank you for getting the bullet out so fast."

"Don't thank me," Daria said. "Thank the gods who watch over shifters that it wasn't lodged somewhere I couldn't get to it."

Max grinned. "I've always been a lucky bastard, and I'm feeling much better. Now go eat your breakfast before it gets cold."

Daria recognized a good suggestion when she heard it and dug into the best meal she'd had in months. Conversation ebbed and flowed around her, but she didn't feel inclined to do much more than listen. Once she was off her feet and shoveling food into her mouth, she realized how depleted she'd become.

"Maybe I'll just check in with the office," Max said.

"In a pig's eye," Johannes shot back.

"Look," Max began. "I understand you'd feel protective—"

Johannes waved him to silence. "We've talked about this before. About arriving at a juncture where you serving as California's governor is too dangerous a charade to continue."

"You're overreacting."

"No. You're underreacting." Johannes got to his feet. "It's time for all of us to move to our headquarters in the Bay Area. At least it's a defensible space. This—" he spread his arms wide "—isn't."

"I agree with Johannes." Max's mate, who'd been mostly silent since Daria began eating, spoke up.

"What's your name?" Daria asked, mostly so she'd have something other than *Max's mate* to call the woman.

"Audrey," she replied, tight-lipped. "And these are my parents, Ron and Bethea Westen."

Daria glanced their way. Ron was a shifter, maybe seventy-five percent pureblooded, and Bethea human. Understanding dawned. Audrey was clearly a shifter, her wolf close to the surface. Since thirty-seven percent blood wasn't enough to shift into anything, she must've been one of the ones who'd taken the serum.

Johannes focused on Daria. "You're done eating. I know I said I wouldn't pump you for data, but Max needs to hear a firsthand account of what happened to our safe house in the South Bay."

"I'm sure that's not necessary," Max muttered.

"Actually, it is." Johannes's voice was soft, but steel sat beneath his words.

Daria tossed back the rest of her coffee. "A call came in about ten hours ago requesting medical assistance. The initial estimate was over fifty wounded, so central dispatch mobilized every one of us in the northern California area. Four teams showed up at what was left of the safe house."

She shut her eyes for a moment, picturing the bombed out mess, the bodies, and the screams of the wounded. Johannes had called it a war zone, and he hadn't been far off the mark. It was indistinguishable from every battlefield where she'd delivered care over the past five hundred years.

"It was probably an inside job since someone used C4 to blow the place up," she went on. "Multiple charges at multiple locations, set to go off at the same time. My team was second on site. Survivors—the ones who could still walk—were sorting wounded to triage."

"How many dead?" Max asked in a strangled-sounding voice.

"Over a hundred. Seventy wounded, but half a dozen died before we could intervene. We transported some to other safe houses—which aren't feeling all that safe at the moment." She leaned her head against the chair's high back. "I'd still be there, but we got the Code Four we were needed here."

"We were planning to go back once we were done," Barney offered.

"We were going to call to see if they still needed us," she corrected him.

"Yes, ma'am." He grinned and poured himself more coffee.

"Do you have a plan once we're at headquarters?" Max asked Johannes. "While we're at it, if that attack happened ten hours ago, why wasn't I notified immediately?"

Johannes crossed his arms over his chest. "Excellent question since I wasn't alerted until I checked in with the vid feed after your attack." He tapped the display on his wrist computer and his face contorted in fury. "There's at least one answer," he ground out. "We weren't alerted because someone's hacked into the vid feed, and they're titrating what comes through. Maybe not exactly titrating, but they're delaying transmissions. Fuck!" Turning, he slammed a fist into the wall. Plaster flaked off.

"Now that we know about it, we can fix it, right?" Max asked. "Surely we can get some of our IT guys on it—"

Johannes cradled his reddened fist in his other hand. "No, what this means is it's even more urgent we get out of here. This morning. We'll lock the place and go."

Max blew out a harried sounding breath. "Which brings me back to my earlier question. Do you have a plan once we get to HQ?"

"Half a one." Johannes narrowed his eyes. "Actually, I've been considering several options we can kick around, once we know for sure who's with us—and how many of us will attempt sabotage from within our ranks."

"Mmph." Max scrunched his face into a frown. "I was hoping this would be clearer."

"You and me both," Johannes muttered. "One part is abundantly clear though, and the bottom line is it's become impossible to keep you safe in such a public role."

Audrey sent a pleading glance across the table at her mate. "Please, Max. We just found each other. It would kill me if anything happened to you."

"Let's talk about this—privately."

He used the table to lever himself to his feet and started for the hall. Audrey raced to his side and looped an arm around his waist.

"A private conversation's a great idea," Bethea said and sent a meaningful glance her husband's way. "Will we stay with Audrey, or should we find our own way? We still have a son to think of."

Ron stood, grim-faced. "How about our room?"

"Perfect." Bethea joined him, and they walked out of the dining room leaning into one another.

"Guess I'll head out to the hovercraft and radio to see if we're still needed in the South Bay," Barney said.

"I could do that." Daria started to get up.

"Nah, I got a head start on breakfast. Grab one of the sweet rolls and have another cup of coffee. I don't nurture you often, Sata. Best soak it up while you can." Breaking into a long-legged lope, he hurried out of the room.

She laughed at his retreating form and murmured, "Truer words were never spoken."

Johannes was still on his feet, hands clasped behind him, staring out a window at a gray day and a cloud-filled sky.

Daria selected a sweet roll and munched the sugar and cinnamon crust, loving the taste of real ingredients on her tongue. "You're worried," she noted between bites.

"No shit," he shot back.

"I still want to know what kind of shifter magic you employed to save your friend."

He spun to face her. "Jesus! You're relentless. We have much bigger problems right now."

"Not relentless. Just curious." She wiped her hands on her napkin and got to her feet. "Even if I'd been here when he was shot, I'm not all that sure I could've saved him. What did you do?"

"Nothing."

The word pinged sourly off her internal compass that sorted truth from falsehood, but there wasn't a way to drag the information out of him. "Maybe someday you'll trust me enough to tell me."

She trotted toward the door and damn near ran into Barney. "They've got things pretty much buttoned up, so we're free until the next call comes in."

They weren't the words she'd hoped for. Not that she wanted to return to the hellhole in the South Bay, but she'd hoped for a straightforward route out of Max's mansion. One where she didn't have to bite her tongue, so she wouldn't call Johannes out for lying to her.

"That's good news," Johannes said, though his tone didn't exactly match the words. "We could use medical personnel at headquarters. The way things stand now, we have to call for assistance just like we did today."

Daria straightened, squaring her shoulders. "I don't take my orders from you."

"If shifters declare martial law, you will. I'm head of security for the underground."

"While you guys duke it out, I'm getting more coffee." Barney scuttled to the table and dug into both the sweet rolls and the remaining coffee. Once he had them in hand, he headed outside. "Let me know when you need me," he told Daria and slipped through a side door, balancing his cup in the crook of one arm.

Johannes's green eyes shaded to a deeper color as he faced her. It might've been a trick of the muted light in the room, but the planes of his face sharpened until he was so striking it was hard to look right at him. And equally impossible to tear her gaze away.

Heat coursed through her, and her belly clenched with long-repressed need. Her breasts felt heavy, the nipples pebbled. If that wasn't bad enough, her cat jumped into the breach. *"Get him for us. He's amazing."*

"Stand down. Not now."

"If not now, then when? All you ever do is work." Grumbly snarls followed the cat's observation.

Daria silently offered her bond animal points for accuracy.

Johannes grinned crookedly, and the tension between them shattered, replaced by something much warmer, but equally hard to come to terms with. "I expected an argument. Instead you're talking with your cat."

Shock mingled with embarrassment. Could he actually hear their conversation? She covered her discomfiture with a question. "How do you know? Most shifters can't tell something like that."

He shrugged. "The gifts manifest differently in each of us."

She was listening carefully. What he'd said was true, but it wasn't the whole story. Not by a long shot. Daria wrenched her eyes from the perfection of his face and sorted through the jumble her thoughts had turned into.

"If you believe you'll need ongoing medical backup, what you need to do is call our central dispatch and—"

"I know our policies," he broke in. "I helped construct them. Not all of our medical personnel are as sharp as you." He took a measured breath. "I can be heavy-handed, not particularly politically correct at times. Would it help if I asked you to accompany us to the underground's headquarters?"

She felt her lips curve into a smile. "Asking always goes down better than telling."

"So if I asked," he persisted, never taking those amazing eyes from her face, "what would you say?"

"That I'd have to square it with medical dispatch. We're short personnel as it is."

He quirked a brow. "Sounds like we're moving toward yes."

"We're actually moving toward maybe." Her smile broadened.

He unclasped his hands and spread them in front of him. "Daria. I'd love it if I had time to court your acquiescence, but once Max shows back up, my priority is getting all of us out of here—especially him. It will take a day or two before Max regains his strength, and I want him in a safe place—at least until then."

"When you floated the idea past Max, you described a permanent move to the underground's headquarters."

"That would be ideal, but if I get enough kick-back from Max, I've found it's good to have a fallback position. He's become surprisingly wedded to his role in human politics, and it's always wise to infiltrate the enemy camp—so long as you can do it without sustaining too many losses."

A snort blew past her lips. "And here you said you weren't politically savvy. That sounded suspiciously like a backup plan to me. One that keeps the mole in place."

"Only a fool doesn't leave a back door open. How about it, Daria? Are you with us?"

"For fuck's sake, say yes," her cat purred from the sidelines. *"That way we'll have a chance to jump his bones."*

"Is your bond animal always this chatty?" Johannes muffled something that sounded like ribald laughter.

Heat swept from her chest to the top of her head, and she knew she was blushing. "Can you hear the words, or just feel the magic?"

"Depends."

"Stop equivocating. Did you hear my cat or not?" Annoyance trumped lust, but it was momentary, and a throbbing warmth settled between her thighs.

"In this particular instance, I heard her, but only because my cat is like-minded and made certain her message came through loud and clear." This time when he looked at her, desire burned in the depths of his eyes, and untapped passion settled between them, igniting the air with the musky scent of a male cat on the prowl.

"Stop. Just stop." She straightened her tired back. "If things are as desperate as I believe they are, this is about the last place ever for a seduction attempt. You're gorgeous, but men like you always know that about yourselves."

"*Shut up,*" her cat snarled, but she ignored it.

Daria forged ahead. "If I talk with dispatch about a semi-permanent assignment at underground headquarters, it has to be with the understanding you won't be hanging around the sidelines leering at me."

"Is that what I'm doing?" His voice was silk, smooth and seductive.

"You know fucking well what you're doing," she growled back. "This conversation just ended. Find another M.D." She spun, intent on tracking Barney down and getting the hell out of there.

Hands settled on her shoulders and turned her roughly. When she stared at him, fierce, raw need was stamped on his face. "Goddammit. Never walk away from me."

She struggled, but his grip was like steel.

"I just did. And I'll do it again once you let go."

"I'll do whatever it takes to get you to come with us. You're beautiful. What man wouldn't want you? And you're a mountain cat, just like me, which makes you even more irresistible." He moved a hand to the side of her face, cradling it and tracing the line of her cheekbone.

This is my chance. Run.

Instead, she nestled into his touch, craving more of it.

"Japanese blood," he murmured. "Asian women have always been my thing, which makes this even harder, but I'll keep my distance. My cat is shrieking his head off. Yours is too, but we'll play this however you want, Daria."

When her name rolled off his lips, it developed a musical cadence that sent shivers cascading down her back. The insidious glow between her thighs brightened until it could've lit a small village.

"Promise?" It was a struggle to get the word out. What she wanted to do was throw her arms around him and crush her aching breasts into his chest. Only part of it was her cat's prodding. The rest was Johannes. She'd never been so attracted to a man in her life.

He nodded and brushed his thumb over her lower lip. "Promise."

"One more thing." Her throat thickened with wanting him.

"What?"

She wrenched out of his grip and took a few steps back. "You haven't answered some of my questions honestly. If we're going to work together, I can't abide liars. If you can't tell me something, just say so. Don't craft something palatable and feed it to me like warmed-over shit."

"Fair enough."

"I'll raise dispatch from the hovercraft. Be back inside once I know something."

Without waiting for him to reply, she hustled out of the room. His scent tickled her sensitive nose, and her body ached for him, but she left anyway. If she didn't put some distance between them, she'd never be strong enough to stay out of his arms.

"He's our mated one," her cat howled in protest. *"Get back in there."*

"Mated one, my ass. You just want to get laid."

A raking sensation burned through her insides. Daria halted just outside the mansion's front door. "Stop that!"

"You will never accuse me of an untruth again. Bondmates never lie to each other."

Guilt flattened her. She'd insulted her cat, her other half. *"I'm sorry. No excuses."*

"Better," her cat growled. *"He is our mated one. I'd never joke about something like that."*

Daria turned the idea over in her head as she made her way to the empty hovercraft. Barney had apparently taken his coffee and rolls elsewhere. Could her cat possibly be right? After almost six hundred years of living, she'd given up on ever finding a mate. Because the hope flaring inside her would lead to crushing disappointment if the cat was wrong, she pushed the whole mess aside and focused on activating the hovercraft's onboard computer to talk with dispatch.

CHAPTER 4

Johannes watched Daria run out of the room. He wanted her with a desperation that surprised him. Usually women were accommodating enough, he didn't waste time on reluctant recruits.

"She's our mate," his cat crowed. *"We finally found her. Get moving. Go after her. Claim her so I can fuck her cat."*

"Even if I believed you, which I don't, you heard her. She was damned clear about a hands-off policy for her to consider coming with us."

"She's just playing hard to get. Once she shifts and her cat and I—"

"Stop it. A few hours ago, you proclaimed we'd never find a mate. Then you said you were done with real, live sex."

"Well, I was wrong."

Johannes pushed his erection to a better position, but it still pressed uncomfortably against his zipper. "Maybe you're wrong this time too. I have more important things to focus on than sex."

Max's chuckle from the hallway reminded Johannes he'd spoken aloud.

"What could be more important than sex?" Max walked into the room, looking quite a bit steadier.

Johannes waved a dismissive hand. At least his libido would stop kicking up hell now. "Well? Are you coming to HQ?"

Max nodded. "Audrey talked me into it. She's packing a few things for us. If I was still alone, I'd likely have argued the point." He skewered Johannes with his icy blue gaze. "I'm not willing to step down from the governor's chair. Not yet."

"How do you envision that working?" Dragging a hand down his face, Johannes dropped into a nearby chair. "If you tell them where you're going, Loren and his crew will insist on coming along. They are your official bodyguards."

"I did consider that."

Johannes waited, but Max didn't say anything else. "Come on." He crooked two fingers. "Spill whatever it is that I probably won't like."

"You know me too well."

"We know each other, and that's not a bad thing. Come on. Give me what we'll be working with, so I can get whatever spin I need to in the pipeline."

Max nodded, and a corner of his mouth turned downward. "I'll drop out of sight. It will take several months for the state to run another election. By then, things will have settled, and if shifters won, I'll show back up, out myself as a shifter, and finish my term."

"Max. This isn't going to take months. The way things have heated up, I'm guessing weeks—maybe as little as a few days—will call it, one way or the other."

"Even better." He walked close and laid a hand on Johannes's shoulder. "I plan to fight until there aren't any of us left—if it comes to that."

"Yeah. I knew that." Johannes stood so he could meet Max's forthright gaze. "I requested a meeting with us and the other ten shifter leaders for later tonight. My message was fully encrypted. Hope it got through. We'll develop our strategy then."

"Excellent. Now that's decided—" Max observed him with eyes that missed very little "—what's up with you and the doc?"

"Nothing."

"Really? It didn't feel like nothing to my wolf—or me."

"Stuff it. She might come with us, but only on the condition I keep to myself. Her exact words were she didn't want me *leering* at her."

"If there's anything I can do…"

"Spoken like a shifter in the throes of mated bliss." Johannes heard the sour undercurrent in his voice and tried to modulate it. "Thanks. You'll be the first to know."

"How are we traveling?" Audrey waked briskly into the room.

"Probably by car. Hovercraft draw undue attention—except for the medical ones with their red crosses on the sides." Johannes snapped his fingers. "That's it. If Daria and Barney come with us, I can use their craft to get you and Max to headquarters. Everyone else can drive."

"Do we know what my parents are doing?" Audrey asked.

Johannes shook his head. "They said something about your brother. Where is he?"

"He's a Sacramento County sheriff. Lives south of the city."

Max frowned. "Is he one of the ones who got the serum?"

"No. Not insofar as I know, anyway," Audrey replied. "He is the one who told me about it, though, so I could be wrong. Do you think he's in danger?"

"We're all in danger," Max said.

"I meant more than most of us because of his connection to me," Audrey clarified.

Ron walked briskly into the room. "Great. You're all here. We just spoke with our son. Bethea and I will spend the next few days there, then he and some of his shifter cronies will meet up with the rest of you in the underground." Ron paused. "He got the injections and is able to shift now too. So he's made a full commitment to our cause."

"Well, that answers one question. What will you be doing after he joins up with the underground?" Audrey asked her father.

"Not sure yet, princess. I'd like to go with your brother, but I don't want to leave your mother by herself."

"She could stay with me."

Ron swept his daughter into a hug and kissed her forehead. "I'll be sure she knows. You have our numbers. We'll be in touch."

"I'm going to try to have everyone out of here by early afternoon," Johannes said, making a stab at diplomacy. It was better than telling Ron that he and Bethea had to get moving pronto.

"No worries on our account," Ron said. "We'll be gone within the next half hour. Never had a chance to really unpack." He shook his head, looking sad. "Last couple years have been hard on Bethea. She really valued having a home, and we've turned into nomads."

"Love you, Daddy." Audrey stood on tiptoe and kissed his cheek.

"Love you too, princess. Got to get back upstairs so I can help your mother carry things down."

"Do you need help?" Max asked.

"Nah, there's not that much. Nomads. Remember?"

Johannes watched him leave. Fury roiled through him. Ron was a decent man. So were ninety-eight percent of the shifters he'd known through his long life. What was happening to them rivaled the worst mankind had to hand out. The Russian pogroms. The Holocaust. Slavery. The Crusades. The Inquisition… Every, single, fucking time, it was some holier-than-thou bastards convinced they had to rid the planet of everyone who wasn't exactly like them.

He refocused. "I'm going to find out what's taking Daria so long." Before Max could make a snide comment, Johannes strode out of the room.

His cat purred hopefully, but remained mercifully silent.

Johannes stopped just outside the door and cast his shifter senses in a wide net. After what happened to Max, it paid to be careful. He assumed the sniper was long gone, but that didn't mean another hadn't taken his place. He searched methodically, but nothing out of the ordinary tripped his senses.

So far, so good.

After discovering they'd been hacked, he didn't trust the vid feed anywhere near the house, but he tapped keys anyway and put in a call to Ryan at underground headquarters.

"Thought I'd hear from you today," Ryan said. His usual jovial manner was absent, replaced by tension that radiated through cyberspace. "What's the plan?"

"Nothing I'm willing to go into until I see you. Any events besides our one safe house?"

"Jesus! Isn't that enough? What a fucking mess."

"I need one of our tech guys here to clean things up. Make sure he has the codes to get inside."

Ryan paused a heartbeat before answering. "Understood. Got it. ETA?"

"Hard to estimate."

"Okay, buddy. Be careful."

"Always."

Johannes disconnected and checked the timer. Thirty-five seconds. Not long enough to trace. He shook himself to dispel apprehension that turned his muscles to rocks. Now was a time to fight, not run. That they had to flee before they could fight went against every instinct.

He jogged toward the hovercraft settled next to Max's larger one. Before he got to it, Barney rose from where he'd been seated leaning against the skids and put a finger over his mouth.

Johannes nodded his understanding and moved silently to Barney's side. The nurse beckoned him around to the hovercraft's open door. Daria was asleep, curled into a ball in one of the craft's four seats. Hair had escaped from her bun; it curled around her face, giving her an innocence that underscored how exhausted she looked. Circles scribed beneath her eyes.

Protectiveness surged, raw and feral. Johannes wanted to erect a barrier around the hovercraft to make certain she could sleep as long as she needed to, yet it wasn't practical.

Barney latched a hand beneath his arm and tugged gently. Johannes followed him about fifty feet from the hovercraft.

"Let her sleep as long as you can," Barney pleaded, keeping his voice soft. "She works harder than any doc I've ever been paired with. Doesn't ever refuse anyone, and it's taken a toll."

"In what way?"

"Her attitude. She used to be positive, at least some of the time. The joy's been bled out of her, but she won't take any time off."

Johannes narrowed his eyes. "You care about her."

"Aw shit, it's worse than that. I love her, but she couldn't care less."

"You've told her."

"More than once, and she blew me off every single time." Barney scrunched his mouth into a tight line. "If I knew what was good for me, I'd ask to be reassigned, but she's great to work with." His voice trailed off. "Anyway, I'd kill if she looked at me like she was looking at you earlier."

Unaccountable pleasure jolted him, but he buried it deep. "Oh really? How was that? I must've missed it."

"That's because she made sure your attention was elsewhere." He shrugged. "She has the hots for you. She probably won't act on it, but you get her going. I'm a shifter too. I can smell arousal from fifty paces. It's one of the reasons I cut and ran with my coffee. Couldn't stand to watch her with you."

"Well, you'll get a long car ride with her." Johannes sidestepped Barney's assessment. "Maybe you can change her mind."

"Not likely. I've been working so closely with her, she strips and changes into fresh scrubs in front of me without batting an eye." He took a breath. "Why will we have a long car trip?"

"Because I'm taking Max and Audrey and the hovercraft to underground headquarters. Medical hovercraft are exempt from regulations. It won't be questioned, and I want to get Max out of harm's way as soon as possible. We have lots of cars here. You can pick what you want to drive."

"Daria got permission for us to join you there, so I'll wake her once I've got a car ready. Maybe that way she'll fall back asleep."

Johannes sent his magic into Barney, probing. At first, he thought the man was a bear shifter, but the energy wasn't quite right, so he upped the ante with his power. What he found startled him. "Son of a bitch. You're an eagle."

The other man nodded. "Guilty as charged. Most people are fooled by my bear disguise, but you drilled right through it. Damned lonely life it's been. I'm pretty certain my parents and their blood kin are the last of our kind, so the only eagle shifters I've ever known were relatives. It makes finding a mate impossible."

"I didn't know any bird shifters remained. You must've kept a pretty low profile."

Barney nodded. "Ravens are truly gone. And there are only maybe twenty eagles left."

Johannes inclined his head. "It's an honor to meet you. I haven't come across a bird shifter in over two hundred years. I'm going to take it as an omen that our kind will prevail."

"Thanks for putting a positive spin on it. Believing good things has to help. Right?"

"Indeed it does."

"Barney. I hear you talking out there," Daria's sleepy voice called from the hovercraft. Moments later, she stepped to the ground and walked slowly toward them.

"Sorry," she addressed Johannes. "Guess I fell asleep after I talked with dispatch. They said it's okay for Barney and me to go to the underground's headquarters—with the caveat that we might get called out from there if we're needed."

"Fair enough." Johannes wanted to hold out his arms and cradle her against him, wanted to smooth the curls back from her sleep-flushed face, wanted to crush his mouth over hers and taste her. Instead, he just drank in her beauty and wished danger wasn't breathing down their backs.

"Do I need to leave?" Barney asked, a meaningful note in his voice.

"Of course not," Johannes answered too quickly.

"Why would you leave?" Daria asked, still sounding out of it. "Won't we be taking off soon?"

"We're driving," Barney told her. "Johannes is taking the hovercraft with Max and his mate."

"Mmph. Guess it makes sense. Except if we're called to an emergency."

"We'll stuff a lot of the medical supplies in the car," Barney said.

Daria brightened. "Good plan. If you figure out what we can drive, I'll make sure the bag has everything we might need."

"On it." Barney slugged Johannes in the arm and said, "Car? Something unobtrusive might shield us from questions if we get stopped."

Johannes thought about it. A vehicle that didn't scream *California governor* would be best, so that excluded the larger, luxury electric cars. "I have just the thing. Follow me, so I can make sure it has a full charge."

Daria turned and trudged back toward the hovercraft.

Johannes didn't want to leave her. Once he recognized that, it stunned him. He headed for the carriage house at a fast trot to cover his uncharacteristic lack of total focus on the problem at hand. Women had never intruded into his work life before—at least not to any significant extent.

"She's our mate. It's why you want to protect her."

"If you want to help," he told his cat, *"be alert for anyone who might want to shoot us out of the skies between here and Hayward."*

He planted his palm on the reader next to the door of the refurbished carriage house that they'd turned into a garage. Once it opened, he made his way to a nondescript, older two seater with a generous trunk. Thank God it was plugged in. He coiled the cord and dropped it in the trunk.

"Looks perfect," Barney said. "I used to have one a lot like this."

Johannes pushed the buttons to operate the overhead door, and it rolled upward. "Take care of Daria." The words tore out of him before he could call them back.

"I could tell you the same thing." Barney's affable expression hardened. "Even though she doesn't want me, if you hurt her, make her any promises that you break, I'll—"

"Don't." Johannes infused strength into the one word. "We have to stand together. If we don't, we won't survive this."

"Sorry," Barney mumbled. "Of course, you're right. I don't have any claim where Daria is concerned. None at all. If she cares about you, I'm happy for her—and for you."

"You're not thinking. I just met her. Yeah, there's an attraction, but we all have much more pressing problems."

Now if I could just get myself to believe that, I'd be in better shape.

Barney opened the door and got into the car. He began tapping data into the onboard nav system.

"Do you know where our headquarters is?"

"Yeah. We treated some folk there last year." Barney flashed him a thumbs-up sign. "See you guys in a couple hours."

The car rolled out of the garage. Johannes started to close the door, then caught himself. He looked for Ron's car to move it outside, but it was already gone.

His wrist computer vibrated, and he glanced at the display.

Ryan.

He accepted the call. "Didn't expect to hear from you."

"Be fucking careful. Take a route they're not expecting."

His screen went blank. Four seconds. Clearly, Ryan wasn't taking any chances.

Johannes bolted for the house. As soon as he was inside, he called for Max, not wanting to take time to hunt him down.

"We're ready." Max and Audrey picked up computer and overnight bags.

"Good." He glanced at Audrey. "Your parents are gone?"

She nodded. "Just left."

Riding on instincts that had rarely failed him, Johannes switched to telepathic speech. *"Go get in the hovercraft. I need to grab a few things from upstairs, then I'll lock up and join you and we'll be gone too."*

Max furled his brows in an unspoken question.

Johannes shook his head. *"Later. Probably better if we don't talk out loud until we're underway."* He bolted up the stairs, taking them three and four at a leap.

Johannes chucked computer equipment, guns, and ammo into duffels and tossed clothes on top of everything. Next came the case holding an assault rifle. That done, he commanded the electronics to wipe every hard drive in the house. It would cost thousands to resurrect everything, but he didn't want to leave the bastards any clues.

He tapped a quick text to Ryan to cancel his earlier request for tech support. No reason to waste manpower on erased drives.

Figuring he'd done all he could, he grabbed what he'd packed and sprinted down three flights of stairs and out the front door, where he activated the most Draconian of the household's alarm sequences. Anyone who set foot in the house would be immersed in poison gas that would kill them almost instantly.

"Take that, you assholes," he muttered and waved a fist skyward.

Feeling almost vindicated after all the trouble humans had caused them, he ran for the hovercraft. Once he was inside, he tossed his duffels and gun case atop Max and Audrey's things in the one empty seat and gave the craft instructions to fly them to Reno.

"What the hell?" Max asked once they were a couple hundred feet in the air. "Hayward's the other way."

"Ryan called. Told me to take an unexpected route."

"But we're in a medical hovercraft," Audrey protested. "Surely…"

"Ssht." Max reached behind his seat and patted her hand. "We'll get there eventually."

Johannes hoped Max was right. He didn't have a good feeling about this trip, but they were safer in the air than on the ground —he hoped.

The radio crackled. "Medevac hovercraft number four-six-three. Flight plan, please."

Johannes groaned. He hadn't counted on air traffic control. Not for a hovercraft flying just above minimums. Where the fuck had they been at dawn today when the bastard had taken a shot at Max?

Audrey tapped his shoulder just before she keyed her mike. "This is Dr. Daria Sata en route to a medical emergency in Reno, Nevada."

"Understood, hovercraft four-six-three. Check in on landing, please."

"Of course." Audrey clicked off. She undid her seatbelt and slithered into the back of the plane.

"What are you doing?" Max asked.

"Hunting for the goddamned transmitter. Need to discombobulate it before we take off again."

"Assuming you locate it, don't touch it until we're on the ground," Johannes cautioned. "Last thing we need is to drop off their radar since someone is obviously interested in this hovercraft."

"I understand." She banged around before crawling back to her seat. "Found it. Looks straightforward to clip the wires."

"Let's think about this," Max said. "Our best bet might be to put down at Reno International where ATC is swamped with traffic. By the time they figure out four-six-three isn't sitting on the tarmac, we'll be long gone."

"No. Audrey told them she was responding to a medical emergency, which means we need to land on one of the helipads on top of a hospital," Johannes countered.

"Or at one of the casinos," Audrey said.

"I like the hospital idea better," Max muttered. "Less likely to be anyone on the roof to see us land and leave immediately afterward."

Johannes figured they'd kick it around between here and Reno. He hoped to hell that wherever they landed, they'd get off the ground with a minimum of fanfare. He didn't want to have to explain why California's governor was traveling incognito in a medical hovercraft.

CHAPTER 5

*D*aria paced from one side of the underground's computer room to the other and back again. She and Barney had arrived an hour ago, and there was still no sign of Johannes, Max, and Audrey.

"I'm sure they're fine," Barney repeated from the console where he had a game up to kill time.

"Well, I'm not," she snapped. "Shit. Sorry, Bar. Didn't mean to sound so short."

The locking mechanism on the door clicked, and Ryan burst inside. Tall, he carried an assault rifle slung over one shoulder. Red hair spilled down his back. Faded Levis and a flannel shirt clung to an impressively muscled frame. Hard, cold, hazel eyes radiated danger.

She'd met him when they arrived—after going through a huge rigmarole that involved actually shifting. When she'd asked why— since she'd been there before—his cryptic reply had been he wasn't taking any chances with anyone.

She leapt to his side. "Did you hear anything?"

Ryan shook his head. He looked like he wanted to kill

something. "ATC was tracking them, but there's no trail after they put down at Reno General Hospital."

"Huh?" Confusion filled her, followed rapidly by fear. "I've never had to file a flight plan with air traffic control for a hovercraft."

"Exactly," Ryan growled. "Hovercraft are normally exempt. My guess is Max and Johannes suspected something was fishy. They must've dismantled the transmitter and taken off again in a hurry."

"That sounds like a good thing." Barney looked up from his simulation. "Like they knew they had to elude the bastards."

"Yeah, but it's a long way from Reno to Hayward. I've run the calculations twice, and I don't think they'd have enough juice to make it without a recharge."

"That's an older hovercraft, and it's not fully electric," Barney said. "It runs on power supplied by an onboard generator, and we had plenty of fuel."

Breath whistled from between Ryan's teeth. "Okay. One less thing to worry about. Johannes is a wizard when it comes to anything mechanical."

"I don't suppose we could ping their wrist computers?" Daria asked.

"Not without compromising them. In the meantime, how about if the two of you come with me, and I can get you settled in the infirmary. There are bedrooms behind it where you can bunk."

Part of Daria perked up; another part groaned. Work. "Does anyone here need a doc?"

"Astute of you. Yeah, there are a couple of injured from that South Bay mess who ended up here. They could use a spot of triage. No one on site here is more than EMT certified."

Barney bolted to his feet and swung their overstuffed medical bag onto his back. "Lead out. Beats playing vid feed games."

Daria ducked under Ryan's arm where he held the door for her. The underground's headquarters was mostly below street level, and she'd visited at least three floors so far. The place was huge. She focused on that to avoid the near panic every time Johannes crossed her mind—which was every few minutes.

What the hell could've happened? Had he, Max, and Audrey been apprehended? Were they being tortured? Hell, they might've even been executed, with no one being the wiser and the bodies cleverly disposed of.

"You lost our mate before we had a chance to bond with him." Her cat's mournful yowl filled her mind, making her feel even worse.

"We don't know he was our mated one."

"Yes," the cat insisted. *"We do."*

Daria didn't have the heart to argue. All she knew was the specter of never seeing Johannes again made her indescribably sad. Even though she recognized it as foolhardy, she wanted to run out of the underground's building and hunt for him.

"If we'd mated with him, you'd be able to find him." Her cat was back with a fury.

Daria knew all about the mate bond. Mates had ways of locating one another through shifter magic, so long as they weren't more than a few miles distant.

But he's not my mate. Just a guy who's too good-looking for his own good—and mine.

"In here." Ryan slapped his palm on a reader next to a door. It opened onto a small, but well-equipped infirmary with men in two beds and a woman in a third one. Three additional beds sat empty. A small lab was set up against the far wall.

Barney dropped the medical bag on a countertop and began making the rounds of their patients. He'd take vitals and let her know who needed her most.

She turned to Ryan. "You said there are living quarters here too."

He nodded. "Through that door are two complete apartments. Come back outside for a moment so I can key your palm print into our system. That way you'll have access to the computer room, the cafeteria, and the infirmary."

She held her hand to the glass while Ryan programmed the

system to accept her. He turned to leave. "Have Barney hunt me down when you guys get a break, so I can do the same thing for him."

"Tell me as soon as you know something," she said, hating the pleading in her voice.

He sent an odd look skittering across the air between them. "All that angst can't be for Max. He's mated. What? You're entranced by Johannes." Ryan exhaled noisily. "He's had hot and cold running women scrabbling for a piece of him as long as I've known the man."

Daria took a chance. "He'd not mated. What about wives or girlfriends?"

Ryan shook his head. "Nope. Never married. Lots of gal pals, but none of them ever made it past his bed into his heart. Not that I'm trying to cut in on his time, but I'm a much safer bet than him. Almost anyone is."

"It sounds like you don't care for him."

"Not true. He's my boss, and I respect the hell out of him. He's a fine strategist and ballsy as all get out. What he isn't is good partner material. He tires of women quickly, and he'll break your heart." Ryan slitted his eyes. "If he hasn't already."

"I barely know him."

"Yeah and just look how worried you are about him. I rest my case. Best advice I have for you is to get in there and take care of your patients. Forget about Johannes."

Daria watched Ryan's retreating back until he disappeared down a stairwell. His words haunted her. Were her feelings for Johannes that misplaced? Not according to her cat.

Almost as if thinking about her bond animal encouraged it, it spoke up. *"I heard all of that. Johannes may have been a lady-killer, but it's only because he never met his mated one."*

"Oh, I suppose once he settles in with a mate, all his bad behaviors will evaporate."

"Of course," the cat replied in a supercilious tone. *"It's the magic of the mate bond."*

Because she didn't want to think about the vagaries of the mate bond, Daria went back inside the infirmary, grateful for something to take her mind off Johannes.

Her nose twitched at the sickly-sweet scent of rotting flesh, and she hurried to Barney. He stood over a young-looking, dark-haired wolf shifter with a hell of a wound in his abdomen. "Didn't get cleaned out before they stitched it," Barney said, his voice carefully neutral.

Daria patted the man's shoulder. "We'll get you fixed up. Barney's going to give you an injection. It'll make you feel dreamy, but shouldn't quite put you to sleep. You won't remember anything, though."

"Probably better that way," the man muttered. "My gut's hurt like a bitch ever since that butcher slapped it shut and stapled it."

She clamped her teeth in a tight line to keep her thoughts on the other side of them. She was pretty sure who'd done the slipshod work on the man. Once he was better, she'd verify it. Maybe if she reported Dr. Weir *again*, dispatch would stop using him.

Catching Barney's eye, she mimicked an injection and he hurried to fill a syringe with Fentanyl mixed with a tranquilizer. She readied a vein and manipulated the tourniquet while Barney injected the man.

The shifter's blue eyes flickered shut, and his breathing became less labored. Daria went to work with Barney handing her what she needed, suctioning the wound, and clearing up blood and pus soaked sponges. She bent close, sniffing, and was finally satisfied she'd cleared out all trace of infection.

"Close him up?" Barney asked.

Daria nodded. "This time, he should be lots more comfortable. He didn't happen to tell you who—"

"He didn't volunteer the information, but I asked." Barney made a sour face. "It was Weir. I swear, that man shouldn't practice on cockroaches, let alone humans."

"I'll mention it to the powers that be, but we're so short of medical personnel, it probably won't do much good. How are the other two?" She jerked her chin at the far corner of the room.

"They're fine. I gave them both sleeping meds. One has burns up one arm from an explosion. The other took a bullet, but it was a clean shot, right through his calf. Nicked the bone, but I checked with the scope and didn't find bone chips."

Half a grin formed on her face. "Remind me again why you didn't go to medical school."

"Couldn't afford it. Being a nurse practitioner is almost as good —until they hand around paychecks."

"No kidding." Daria knew how pathetically little she made, and his salary was only about seventy percent of hers. "I'm going to check out our digs."

"I already did. I took the room on the left, but I'm good with either one. They're almost exactly the same. We share a bathroom."

"We can probably manage that. So long as you remember to leave the lid down."

Barney snorted laughter. "I'll give it my best shot."

A fast glance at her wrist computer told her another hour had ticked by. One more hour with no word about Johannes. Tension carved a line through her from her skull to her toes. She looked at her new bedroom—bland, but serviceable—and fell onto the bed rubbing her forehead to counteract the headache pounding behind her temples.

She shouldn't care whether she ever saw Johannes again. They barely knew each other. The tumult churning her guts to mush didn't make sense, but she couldn't reason it out of existence. If something hideous happened and he never came back, she wasn't certain she'd ever get over it.

"Oh for Christ's sake, get a grip," she muttered.

Deep inside her, the cat concocted a snarly purr, but stopped shy of nattering about the mate bond again.

~

JOHANNES HOVERED, letting the craft's skids barely kiss the rooftop landing pad of Reno's largest hospital. His heart beat hard against his ribs, and his mouth flooded with the metallic taste of too much adrenaline. His cat wanted out, but it understood it would only be in the way in the hovercraft cockpit.

"Done," Max said to the accompaniment of breaking glass. He and Audrey were busy disconnecting and disabling the beacon that blipped their position on ATCs radar. "Give it sixty seconds for any residual transmissions to die, and then we can leave."

A quick glance out the windscreen convinced him no one had come scooting through the doorway to greet them and escort whatever gravely ill patient they were delivering to either the E.R. or intensive care.

If nothing changed in the next few seconds, they'd escape undetected. He willed the goddamned hospital door to stay shut and even sent a jot of shifter magic to seal it. All it would create was a minor inconvenience if someone was on the other side, but he'd take all the help he could get.

He fed power from the generator to the motor and they lifted smoothly into smoggy skies. If he got high enough, they could hide in the smog, but that would take time, and right now speed was their friend. The faster they got clear of Reno's airspace, the better their chances of eluding discovery.

Max fell into the co-pilot's seat, and Johannes heard the snap as Audrey buckled into hers. "I'll feel safer after we have at least twenty minutes lead time," Max said.

"You and me both," Johannes replied. Breath rasped in his throat, and his stomach burned, twisting into a hard knot of tension.

"Is it because the circle where we might be grows larger with each minute that passes?" Audrey asked.

"That's exactly it," Max said. "The bigger head start we get, the more territory they'll have to search to pinpoint our location. Once they determine we eluded their net."

"And that's also why I'm heading due west from here," Johannes said. "If they suspect who's in this craft—and they'd almost have to since they're tracking us—they'll expect us to head for the Bay Area. I'll wait until I'm close to the ocean at the edge of the Bay Area corridor to head south."

"Good fucking thing this sucker runs on a gas-powered generator," Max muttered.

Johannes didn't bother to answer. If they'd been in one of the newer, all-electric models, they'd have been royally hosed. Luck had been with them so far. He breathed a silent prayer it would last.

As if Max had read his mind, he said, "Eleven minutes."

"Good. Keep track and let me know at the five minute markers."

Twenty-five minutes into their getaway from Reno, Johannes felt his breathing normalize. He'd passed the crest of the Sierras and was heading into thickly forested foothills. If need be, he could land, and the forest canopy might hide them.

"We should've brought more weapons," Max said.

"Knowing you—" Johannes cast a sidelong glance his way "—you didn't leave home empty-handed."

"Not entirely."

"Neither did I."

"I have my brother's laser pistol," Audrey offered.

Johannes snorted. "The better I get to know you, the more I like you."

Max preened under the compliment about his mate. "She truly is amazing. Bright, beautiful, brave, enterprising."

"Enough!" Audrey bent forward to grasp Max's shoulder. "I'll become insufferable."

"That could never happen, darling." He reached up and squeezed her hand.

Their joy was so palpable, Johannes wished he could bottle the emotion and feed off it.

"You don't need to. Our mate's at underground headquarters," his cat said snidely.

Max perked up. "I heard that. Your cat thinks Daria is your mate."

"My cat's just lonely," Johannes mumbled.

"My wolf was convinced about Max long before I was," Audrey said, followed by, "Shit! What's that?"

Johannes followed her finger and saw another hovercraft flying about the same elevation, heading southeast. This one lacked any sort of identifying insignia, but they were outside city airspace, so hovercraft were allowed. It was too late to alter their flight trajectory. The other craft had to have seen them, and it would certainly notice.

"Duck," he hissed at Max. "Or at least cover your hair."

"Here." Audrey passed her sweater forward, and Max draped it around his head to cover his telltale white-blond hair.

Playacting to the hilt, Johannes caught the other pilot's eye when the two craft passed one another and nodded affably. The other man gave him a thumbs-up sign...and kept flying.

"It's all right," Audrey said. "Thank fucking Christ they weren't hunting for us."

"We don't know that for sure," Johannes cautioned. "I'm going to put us down north of the highway, and Max and I will do what we can to cover up the red crosses on both doors."

"Solid plan." Max thumped Johannes's arm. "Ashamed I didn't come up with it first. When Audrey and I were mucking around in the back, we found rolls of old silver duct tape."

"Better and better." Johannes grinned. "We should be able to cover those telltale markings in jig time, and the tape will almost match the hovercraft. Hang on, we're landing over there." He nodded toward an opening in the trees.

"But won't we need the medic markings once we're back over urban airspace?" Audrey asked.

"Yes and no," Max answered. "They'd help for that part of the trip, but for right now being invisible will be safer."

Covering the crosses didn't go quite as fast as Johannes hoped it would. The tape didn't stick very well to the craft's aluminum sides until Audrey got the idea of sluicing them with ethanol—a medical supply item the craft had plenty of. By the time they were airborne again, it was getting dark.

Silence settled in the cockpit while Johannes navigated to the ocean's edge and turned them south. He'd done some angling prior to that, so they wouldn't have quite so far to fly over the urban sprawl beneath them. Not all of it was city airspace, but enough of it was that this last part of the journey was even dicier than their maneuver in Reno.

"Both of you keep an eye out," Johannes cautioned. "I'm running without lights."

"You got it," Audrey said, but she sounded trashed.

Johannes didn't blame her. It had been a hell of a day. First Max's near brush with death, then their precipitous flight, and now crowded, urban airspace where hovercraft were definitely illegal. The medical insignia would've bought them a lot—if someone wasn't hunting for a craft with just those markings.

By now whoever was after them had to have pulled out all the stops. The last fifteen minutes until he settled the craft on the roof at the underground's headquarters aged him fifteen years.

"Shit!" He uncramped his fingers from around the controls, flexing them. "I've never been so happy to get out of the air."

"It was a bit on the nerve-wracking side," Max agreed. "I expected to be shot down any minute."

"We just found each other," Audrey said. "Nothing will part us."

Because Johannes was sitting next to Max, he saw complex

emotions cross the other man's face before his features settled into a fierce desperation. Being on the run didn't suit Max's temperament any better than it suited his own. And now Max had a mate to protect.

The roof door swooped open. Ryan and Devon launched themselves at the craft, pulling its door open. "It's about fucking time," Ryan growled.

"Better late than never," Max quipped and got out of his seat. He helped Audrey up, and the two of them exited the bird. "We'll stop by the cafeteria, and then I'm taking Audrey to my quarters," he told Ryan.

"I'll be in just as soon as I've caught up with Johannes."

"We'll see your stuff gets to you," Devon added.

"What time was that war council?" Max asked Johannes.

"Crap!" Johannes looked at his wrist computer. He'd totally forgotten about setting it up. "Not for ninety minutes. Thank God."

"If I don't run into you before then," Max said, "I'll see you in the conference room." He herded Audrey toward the open door and disappeared inside.

"You have no idea how narrowly you eluded disaster," Devon said.

"How close were they?" Johannes wasn't certain he wanted to know.

"Breathing down your ass. If you hadn't left Reno immediately, the trap would've snapped shut. Somehow, they knew Max was in that hovercraft."

"I'm still blown away you actually made it here," Ryan muttered. "We were about to send out trackers. In case you'd gone to ground somewhere."

"We did for a little bit." Johannes dragged his body out of the hovercraft and pointed to its sides. "Covered up the red cross insignia."

"Smart." Devon nodded. "It's the small shit that trips people up, and they were likely fixated on medical hovercraft."

"Probably the only reason you slipped through their net," Ryan agreed.

"I'm still trying to figure out how they knew Max was even traveling." Johannes forced his tired mind into motion.

"That one's easy," Ryan cut in. "They were monitoring your house through the vid feed."

"I put an end to that by killing all the drives."

"This time," Devon snarled darkly.

"Max can't ever go back there. Not until this is over." Ryan's voice rang with determination.

"I think he gets that," Johannes said. "Finally. For a little bit there earlier, I wasn't at all certain I'd pry him out of Sacramento. He *likes* being the state governor."

"What made the difference?" Devon asked.

"Audrey."

Devon's stark, Native American features broke into an uneasy grin. "Damn mate bond. Works every time."

"Speaking of which—" Johannes eyed him "—where's Kate?"

"Working the communications vectors. I should get back to her. See you at the meeting."

Johannes turned back toward the craft. "How about if you take Max and Audrey's stuff with you?"

"Sure." Devon shouldered past him and grabbed all the bags.

"Those are mine." Johannes levered them from his grip.

"Want me to have some dinner sent to your room?" Ryan asked.

"Nah. I don't need you to wait on me. I'm going to take a shower, and then I'll catch a bite before the meeting."

Motion in the stairwell shot his hackles to full alert until his cat purred. *Our mate is on her way. She knows she's ours. Even if you don't.*

Ryan shot him an odd look. "I'm out of here, dude. See you soon."

Daria burst through the door, almost running squarely into Ryan. Her hair was loose, dark curls falling halfway to her waist. Her dark eyes gleamed with pleasure—and relief. "You're back. My cat said you were, but I didn't see how she could've known..." Her voice ran down, and she stood gazing at him, yearning quivering from every pore.

"Go to her," his cat urged. *"Make her ours."*

Johannes stopped thinking. He dropped his bags and closed the distance between them, crushing his mouth over hers. She kissed him back with a fervor to match his own. Their tongues sparred, and he sucked in the sweetness of her. Her body turned to scorching, liquid lust in his arms, and she made hungry, mewling sounds. Hands splayed across his back tugging him closer, and he hugged her back. The rightness of Daria in his arms, breasts smushed against his chest, rocked him to his core. He cradled her head between his hands, sinking his fingers into all her glorious hair, and deepened their kiss.

His cock rose between them, and he thrust his hips forward to maximize the contact between their bodies.

"Hate to intrude, man, but you've got to come now." Devon's deep voice cut through Johannes's total concentration on the woman folded against him.

A cold splash of reality followed on the heels of Devon's words. Nothing had changed. No matter how attracted he was to Daria, he couldn't loose the brakes and let himself care about her. It would come back to bite him in the ass when she eventually died, and he had to go on—alone.

No. The only women for him were for one purpose only. Sexual release. Sex with Daria would cut to his soul, and he couldn't risk it. He let go of her, abruptly moving away. "I'll meet you in the com room," he told Devon.

"Got it. Make it snappy. There's something you've got to see." Devon turned, vanishing down the stairs.

"Did I do something wrong?"

Daria turned her liquid gaze on him, and his heart ached for all the missed opportunities and might-have-beens in his life. She reached for him, but he shook his head.

"What?" she persisted. "My cat believes you're our mate."

"Do you?" The words left his lips before he could hold them back.

She smiled softly, and his heart shattered with wanting her.

"I don't know, but we owe it to ourselves to find out."

"Do not fuck this up," his cat chimed in. *"Make her ours. It's more important than whatever Devon wanted."*

Johannes felt as if he was being ripped in half. Duty on the one hand and desire so strong it filled every molecule of his being with white-hot need on the other.

"I don't have time for this," he growled. He'd meant to use telepathic speech and answer his cat, but he was tired.

The words sat between him and Daria as if he'd inscribed them in the air with black paint. The wounded look that bloomed on her face smote him. Before he could tell her he hadn't meant it the way it sounded, she spun on her heel and ran down the stairs.

CHAPTER 6

$\mathcal{D}$aria was amazed she made it to the bottom of the flight of stairs without falling. Her eyes flooded with tears. They fell thickly, obscuring her vision. Beyond emotional pain that flayed her raw, she was angry with her cat.

"Why? Why'd you tell me he was back and push me to find him?" she demanded and then switched to telepathy. *"He doesn't want us— or anyone. Ryan was right about him. He's just a fuck 'em and leave 'em type."* The impact of her words sank in and she followed them with, *"If Devon hadn't shown up, we'd be the latest in Johannes's list of conquests. No more. No less."*

"You're wrong," the cat replied, but she sounded sad. *"If you'd made love, you'd have shifted, and then everyone would know the truth. That you're mates."*

Daria ducked into a doorway to avoid two men racing down the hallway. Apparently, something had happened, and everyone was in a hell of a hurry. At least she'd avoided whatever path Johannes took after he followed Devon to the central communications room. Since the only places she could find were the cafeteria, computer room, and infirmary, she'd made a lucky guess at a route where she wouldn't have to see him again.

At least not quite so soon.

I don't have to see him ever again. I can rustle up Barney. We'll contact dispatch and tell them we're heading home, and we'll be available from there next time they call.

Her heart ached—assaulted by tiny, sharp shards of broken hopes—but leaving was by far the soundest strategy. She got her bearings and walked briskly toward the infirmary. No one there needed onsite medical personnel. No reason she couldn't leave immediately.

"*You can't go,*" her cat protested.

"*Watch me.*"

"*It's a mistake.*"

Daria ground to a halt. *"Now you look here. I understand you're convinced he's our mate, and I'm telling you even if he is, I don't want him. Not now. Not ever. Got it?"*

Her cat didn't answer. When Daria looked within, the animal had withdrawn. They had a place they went when they needed a break. A relieved breath rattled through her lungs. Not arguing with her cat would be a big plus as she finessed getting herself and Barney out of there. She didn't want to ask for a vehicle because she didn't want Johannes to plant himself in front of her and order her to stay.

Not that he would at this point, but she still didn't want to see him.

That meant she and Barney would have to rely on getting to one of the central transportation hubs. Probably not too difficult. She'd noted one only half a dozen blocks to the north when they drove in. As an M.D. she wasn't worried about authorities creating problems for her. Medical personnel were in such short supply, no one wanted to get on their bad side. And she did just enough work for humans—in between her assignments from shifter dispatch—to let them believe she was one of them.

A few more strides brought her to the infirmary door. She pushed her way inside and stopped dead. What had been three beds with mostly well patients had turned into a fucking zoo. The other three beds were full, and men and women lay moaning on cots and on the floor. A quick count tallied twenty-two crammed into the smallish space.

Barney's head snapped up. "It's about goddamned time. I couldn't leave here to find you. Asked someone I didn't know to hunt you down... Doesn't matter. I'm losing this one, Sata. See what you can do."

Daria dove to her knees beside the comatose woman. A coyote shifter, she'd lost a lot of blood, and half her face was burned down to bone. Even though she was out cold, a keening moan issued from her throat. "What'd you give her?" she asked Barney.

"Opiates, but not too much. I was afraid I'd kill her. She keeps trying to shift, but can't gin up enough magic."

"Shifting might be a good thing. Her coyote heals faster. Failing that, her animal won't want her to die in human form."

"The transformation takes two of us," he reminded her. The censure in his tone needled her about her absence from their joint workstation, but he stopped short of asking where she'd been.

"How about the rest of them?" She swept an arm to encompass the room. "Will anyone else die if we take a few minutes to help coyote gal here shift?"

Barney drew his red brows together. "A couple are critical, but if we wait, this one will die for sure."

Daria nodded sharply. "Ready when you are."

They joined hands over the coyote woman's body and began the ancient chant to draw her animal form into ascendency. This was a type of healing Daria had known and used before modern time, long before she'd gone through medical school. Her blend of old and new methods was a boon. It gave her an arsenal today's human practitioners couldn't even dream about.

Paws formed on the coyote. Daria gripped one to anchor it and called for her cat to return and help her. The animals had their own network, and if anyone could help, it would be her cat—or Barney's eagle. Both bond animals formed in her mind's eye, and the body beneath her hands shimmered, but didn't shift.

Daria poured power into her working and felt an infusion from Barney. Finally, when sweat ran down her sides, the air solidified, and a coyote with soft, gray fur lay on its stomach, panting softly.

"The coyote thanks you," her cat advised her in formal tones that meant she was still angry.

"Tell her to stay alive, goddammit," Daria muttered.

"Even if her human doesn't survive, you've freed the coyote from a living hell." A measured pause. *"I love you for it, bondmate, but I still think you're making a mistake about Johannes."*

Before she could answer, her cat vanished from her mind.

Barney grabbed a sponge and swiped it across his forehead. "That's all we can do here. Our animals will sit with the coyote."

Daria understood triage. "Who's next?"

Barney got to his feet. "Bear shifter back in the corner."

Daria followed him. "What happened to all of these shifters? Was there another attack?"

Glancing over his shoulder, Barney nodded, his eyes sad—and angry. "These were all part of the group of shifters who just emerged from hiding. Someone ratted them out, so the new network of safe houses the underground developed as a stopgap were booby-trapped. Opening the front door activated bombs that blew anyone who walked through them to Hell."

She swallowed hard. "Don't we usually have resident gatekeepers at our safe houses?"

"You're usually smarter than that, Sata." He looked away, but fury sheeted from him in visible waves.

"Shit. The gatekeepers were either part of the rogue network, or easy enough to corrupt with bribes."

"I don't know for sure, but it's close to the conclusion I came to."

She slid to a sit next to the barely breathing bear shifter. "Goddammit! How many died?"

Barney positioned himself on the other side of the bear. "We don't know. Last estimate I heard, over a hundred. We got the survivors—some of them anyway. Others went to various original, trustworthy safe houses that are still standing."

Daria ran practiced hands over the inert body in front of her, and sent magic after her touch, fixing what she could. Her mind raced. How much longer could any of them survive? Humans outnumbered them. In any kind of confrontation, shifters would lose because of sheer numbers.

I can't think like that.

Yeah, better if I don't think at all. I don't like any of the answers.

Even though she recognized she was retreating to survival mode, she narrowed her focus until the only thing in her mind was the man on the floor in front of her struggling to live.

"Where were you earlier?" Barney's question was quiet, so quiet she almost missed it. They'd stabilized the bear and moved on to a female wolf.

"If doesn't matter. I was nowhere."

"If you want to talk about it—"

"I don't. Mix up some antiseptic solution so we can clean this wound."

"Jesus, Sata. I was trying to be supportive."

"Don't be anything except my partner in crime saving lives." She tossed him a weak smile that cost her because the last thing she felt like was smiling.

"Got it. Give me a few. We burned through our own supplies, and I'm not certain where the replacement crap is in here."

She glanced at him, but he was on his feet and moving away. From the uber-straight set to his shoulders, she knew she'd hurt his feelings, but she couldn't stand to talk about Johannes. Ever. This latest wrinkle delayed their departure from the shifter underground's headquarters, but it didn't mean they weren't leaving as soon as they could.

∾

JOHANNES STOOD behind a console watching one hideous scene after another roll in on the vid feed. Before he arrived, Ryan and Devon had deployed every available operative to find and offer sanctuary to the remaining shifters who'd come out of hiding, only to walk into traps.

"Bastards did this on purpose," Johannes said through gritted teeth.

"You bet," Max agreed from where he sat in front of his own console across the room. "They want to make it look like we sabotaged our own kin. Lured them out into the open and then fucked them over."

"This is going to turn into a full on war," Devon snapped.

"It already has," Ryan noted. "No *going to* about it."

"Bastards deserve it, after what they're doing to us." Kate's stunning face was set in harsh lines. Her red-gold curls had been drawn back into a messy queue. A mountain cat shifter, she was Devon's mate.

"It's almost time for the meeting," Max noted.

Johannes nodded and worked the vid feed to funnel in the other ten shifter leaders. They'd always been governed by a dozen from countries all over the world. Long ago, they'd communicated telepathically, but electronics changed all that. There was too much interference from all the wireless signal patterns for them to reach one another that way anymore. Absent telepathy, the vid feed worked. It wasn't as secure, which worried Johannes, but there wasn't shit he could do about it on short notice.

Daria scuttled through his mind, but he blocked her out. Her scent still lingered, tickling his nostrils, and the memory of the feel of her in his arms ignited his senses.

Stop! Not now. This meeting requires my full and absolute attention. We're dying. If we don't do something radical, there won't be any of us left.

Except me.

Screens flickered to life around the room. It didn't take long to ascertain that the primary focus of the attacks was in the U.S.

"That's good news," Max noted, narrowing his eyes to slits. "Johannes won't like this, but I'm going back to Sacramento. I have an idea that might fix this once and for all, but I need the power of the governor's office to pull it off."

"I don't fucking think so," Ryan and Johannes said almost in unison. Both men jumped to their feet and stood over Max as if they could hold him in his seat by sheer force of will.

"Let us at least hear what he has to say." Boris, another Russian wolf shifter with steel gray hair and gray eyes, said from the vid feed.

"СПАСИБО" Max thanked the other shifter in Russian.

He shut his eyes for a moment. After he opened them, he straightened in his chair. "I'm going to blow the lid off the hush-hush murder of shifters in our jails and prisons nationwide. I have all the top-secret reports. I've been saving them, not shredding them. I also have the reports about how they tortured us—before they started killing us to save time."

"They will discredit you," Boris said quietly.

"It's hard to discredit facts," Max countered.

"They'll say you manufactured them," Johannes said, still aghast Max was considering putting himself squarely in the line of fire. "You're newly mated. Think of Audrey."

Max shifted his unsettling blue eyes to Johannes. "I am thinking about her. And about every other shifter in the U.S. And the world. If we don't put a stop to this here, it's only a matter of time before the rest of you—" he glanced at the vid feed screens "—are faced with the same problem."

"A sniper almost killed you this morning," Johannes argued. "If Audrey hadn't found me as fast as she did—"

"I know what you did." Max shielded his mind voice and aimed it only for Johannes.

"I'm sure I have no idea what—" Johannes blustered, though it was hard to pull off with telepathy.

"Cut the shit. My wolf told me. I'm like you now. We're bonded by blood, and I can't die. Don't worry. I'll guard your secret."

Johannes couldn't wipe the shocked look off his face fast enough the others didn't notice. He clicked his jaw shut, his mind whirling a million miles an hour.

"Whatever is passing between you should be out loud so the rest of us can hear," Boris said.

Max shook his head vehemently. "No. It shouldn't."

Johannes felt like he'd been kicked in the guts. How could Max's wolf have figured out something even he didn't know? He'd aimed to help Max, not turn him into a clone.

"You didn't know because you've never used your blood to save anyone before," his cat piped up. *"Max's wolf is smart. I tried to kick him off the scent trail earlier, but he wasn't buying it."*

Truth flattened Johannes—followed rapidly by trepidation. He expected Ceres's wrath to surface any moment. Why it hadn't already was a mystery. He'd broken the covenant between them. Not intentionally, but the net effect was the same.

"Johannes?" Max gripped his hand hard. "We need you here. You and I can talk about the other later. Or not at all. Your choice."

"Of course." Johannes buried everything but the front-and-center present. He'd had lots of practice. It wasn't even all that hard. He'd turned *I'll think about it later* into almost as staunch an art form as his masturbation videos. The comparison brought a sardonic smile to his face.

"Moving forward," Max went on smoothly. "I'll wait until tomorrow, and then I'll show up at my office. Ryan, Devon, and Johannes can be my bodyguards in addition to my set crew at the capitol. It will take me a couple hours to get the information into a coherent package, and then I'll start running it through every vid feed in the country. I'll need a couple of our tech guys with me to make sure the channels remain open."

"I do not like it," Carlos, a cat shifter from Argentina, said in heavily accented English. "They could kill you while you are transmitting."

"They'd have to get into my office first." Max barked harsh laughter. "The place is bulletproof and bombproof, designed to withstand a siege."

"Where will Audrey be?" Johannes asked.

"That's why I'm not leaving until tomorrow." Max glanced away. "I'd like her to remain here, but I'm betting she gives me grief over it. My wolf isn't on board with leaving her here, either."

"It'll be three against one," Kate said smugly. "If Devon's going with you, so am I. Mated couples are never parted."

Max rolled his eyes. "You've been a shifter for over three hundred years, Ms. Roman. Audrey doesn't know shit about how to keep herself safe. Hell, she's barely learned how to shift."

"I have some thoughts," Boris cut in. "Each of us can mobilize an elite force of, say, five hundred. That will be five thousand in aggregate. We can travel to Sacramento and put a hell of a hole in any sort of opposition camped outside your office waiting to blow you to bits if you so much as poke your head out."

Boris's words warmed Johannes. Shifters were some of the most amazing creations on Earth. Why anyone would target them eluded him. Being different wasn't cause for genocide. Wiping out shifters would not make the world a safer place. Quite the opposite.

"...kind of you, but I don't want you to put yourself and your men at risk," Max was saying when Johannes refocused on him.

"Bullshit," Carlos muttered. "It is not kind. It is self-serving. The world must see there are many of us, and that we protect our own." He turned his attention to the others. "Who is in?"

A chorus of assent rose.

"And so that is settled," Boris said in a satisfied-sounding voice. "We need to integrate with your timeframe. For us to get there, we will need more than a few hours lead time. It is early Tuesday morning here, still Monday where you are. I recommend you wait until Friday so we can all get into position."

"Done," Max said. "Whether I show up Tuesday or Wednesday or Friday won't make a whole hell of a lot of difference. I'll just get into position a few hours ahead of time to get my vid feed idea rolling."

"Stand firm, *mis hermanos*," Carlos said. "My brothers. We are family. We will not lose this war."

The other shifter leaders offered assent and support before vid screens winked out. If their situation weren't so desperate, Johannes would look forward to seeing everyone. They hadn't all been physically present in one place since before computers were invented.

"What would it take for you to change your mind?" Ryan walked to Max's side. "We need you to run the underground."

"If this works—" Max inhaled sharply "—we won't need the underground anymore. We'll be free again."

"If it doesn't," Ryan persisted, "who will take your place?"

"None of us are irreplaceable." Max got to his feet. "It will work, though. I'm not in the habit of tying my star to the losing pony."

Johannes grinned in spite of himself. When Max quirked a brow his way, he shook his head. He didn't want to talk about what Max revealed. Not yet. He needed to think it through first. Since no one needed him, he ducked out of the room and made his way one floor up to his spartan bedroom. A single bed sat against one wall. A computer desk against another. His bags were where he'd left them, dead center on the floor. Community bath facilities were located down the hall. Bending, he picked up his duffels and assault rifle case and chucked them into the closet.

He'd never expected to spend much time at the underground HQ, so having more comfortable quarters wasn't high on his agenda. Too tense to sit, he paced from one side of his room to the other, then back again. If his blood could confer the gift of immortality on other shifters, they'd truly become invincible.

Yes, but how much blood?

And if he consciously created more like himself, would it truly piss Ceres off?

The goddess hadn't shown up after his transgression this morning. Did she even know what had happened?

If she knows, does she care anymore?

An amazing thought slammed into him—a veritable miracle—and he stopped pacing. He could share his blood with Daria. The blood bond would make her immortal and—

"No. That's wrong. Just fucking wrong." He spoke aloud to steady himself.

"It's not wrong to make certain your mated one shares your immortality," his cat spoke up. *"It's the rightest thing in the world."*

"You make it sound easy."

"It is easy," his cat persisted. *"You're the one making it hard."*

Johannes played back what happened earlier with Daria and winced. "Hell, I'll be lucky if she ever talks to me again." He waited, but his cat didn't pop off with a snappy comeback.

Without fully realizing his intent until he stood over the vid screen, he tapped into feeds from all over the underground's headquarters. Daria was in the infirmary, right where he expected to find her. The number of patients scattered about was disturbing, but not unexpected given the magnitude of today's attacks.

Feeling guilty and like a spy, he watched her for long moments as she moved from patient to patient. Her scrubs were splattered with blood, and she looked tired, but she was still working, bending over wounded to treat them. Somewhere between her rooftop visit and now, she'd braided her dark hair, and it hung down her chest in two thick plaits.

His heart went out to her. He wanted to drag her out of the infirmary and see she got a meal and a few hours' sleep. He wanted to fuck her senseless too, but that would have to wait until they got things between them squared away.

If squaring away was even possible at this point.

His comment about not having time had hurt her. She fairly oozed pride, and he didn't think she'd forgive him easily. Maybe not at all. It must've taken a lot for her to approach him, emotions wide open, and he'd tossed her gift aside as if it meant nothing.

It looked like she and Barney were arguing about something, so he activated the audio channel.

"I agree we're not done here," she said, "but once we are, we're leaving."

"Why? I thought this was our new assignment."

"I'm not talking about why, I'm telling you what is. You work for me. I work for dispatch. Haven't had time to clue them in, but there's a transport hub not far from here—"

"Oh ho! I get it. You had a fight with lover boy, and now we're sneaking out of here like—"

Daria narrowed her eyes. "Shut up. I will not discuss this. Shit!" She exhaled noisily. "You're as bad as my cat. At least she's busy with the coyote right now."

"Coyote gal will make it," Barney said. "My bird told me the crisis had passed a few minutes ago. Okay, Sata. I won't mine for any more details. But I know you better than anyone, and you look like hell. Make very certain it's what you want before we cut and run."

"It is," she said tight-lipped.

Johannes had heard and seen enough. He turned off the vid feed and hurried from his room, intent on dragging Daria out of the infirmary at least long enough to apologize. If she was still listening, he'd explain himself. Or try to. The words wouldn't come easy since he'd never shared what he was with anyone. It wasn't even a conversation he had with his cat very often.

None of that mattered. What did was Daria. If he didn't do something, she'd run from him and cover her tracks so she'd be damned hard to find.

CHAPTER 7

*D*aria had just finished setting a broken arm when the snick of the infirmary door opening settled into her gut like a lead weight.

Crap! More patients, and she was beyond weary.

A startled intake of breath from Barney brought her to her feet, and she raked the room hunting for who the new arrivals might be. If something startled him, it must be pretty bad.

Her gaze lit on Johannes, and her heart squeezed painfully, making her chest hurt. "What?" she inquired dully. "We're here. We're working. What else could you possibly want?"

He glanced around the room, and she felt the flash of his power, no doubt feeling for life energy from her various patients. "I need to talk with you, Daria. No one is so ill you can't leave for a few minutes."

"I'll keep watch," Barney spoke up. "We were pretty much done with everyone."

Daria shot daggers his way. Last thing she needed was the path cleared for her to have some one-on-one time with a man she never wanted to see again. She squared her shoulders and stared at Johannes. "If you need something from me, call dispatch."

He narrowed his eyes. "But you're right here."

"Observant of you." She let acid etch into her words. "I don't want to talk with you—about anything. You had your chance. You blew it big time. This is my space. Get out of here."

Johannes exchanged a look with Barney. Something passed between them, and Barney walked past her and on out the door. "Wait!" she called after him. "You can't leave."

Ignoring her words, he said, "I'll be in the cafeteria."

She ground her teeth together until her jaws ached. "Just because you bullied him into leaving—"

"I did no such thing." Anger flashed from Johannes's oh-so-green eyes. "He recognized we need to clear the air, so he offered us an opportunity."

"I don't give a fuck what he did. I have nothing to say to you. Nothing. Make it easy on both of us, and go back to saving the world for shifters." She turned away, hoping against hope he'd get the hell out of her infirmary.

Footsteps moved to her side. The warmth of him seared her, but he didn't lay hands on her. Part of her was grateful, the other part disappointed. She hated the welter of conflicting emotions churning her guts to bits.

"I'm sorry, Daria. I made a mistake. In truth, I've made bunches of them, but I never meant to hurt you."

Apparently, she couldn't get rid of him that easily. She turned slowly and looked at him. "Are you done? If you are, the door's that way." She pointed, but he didn't move, just looked at her, something unreadable on his face. "Look." She sucked air and went on. "I can't leave. These people still need me, but as soon as they don't, Barney and I will be out of here."

"I don't want you to leave."

"And I don't care what you want. It's good I was here, but you can get another doc from dispatch. That's actually a good idea. I'll raise them right now, and as soon as my replacement shows up..." She bent over her wrist computer and began tapping buttons.

Johannes placed the flat of one hand over the display and grabbed her wrist with the other. "Goddammit. I want to talk with you."

"You apologized. I've accepted. We're done." She couldn't look at him. Had to get him out of her space. If she didn't, she'd end up back in his arms. A place that spelled danger with a capital D.

"If you accepted my apology—and you never actually said that except by inference right now—why are you trying to force me out of here?"

"Because there's no reason for you to stay." She looked within, searching for her cat, but the animal wasn't there. Probably a good thing. If she was, she'd only make things harder.

He tilted her chin up with a finger so she had to look at him. What she saw in his eyes gave her pause. Pain and need vied with guilt for ascendency.

"Hear me out, please. If you still want me to leave afterward, I promise I will."

"Fine. Anything that gets you out of here." She winced at the harshness in her words, but if she didn't stand firm, she'd be lost.

He nodded. "I'm going to shield us so anyone who might be conscious can't hear. It's easier than telepathy, and I want access to my voice. It reflects emotion better than mind speech."

She jerked her chin away from his finger and motioned for him to get on with it. The sooner he said whatever was in his head, the sooner she could put her wounded heart back together. She still didn't quite understand why breathing the same air as him made her long for him beyond the dictates of common sense.

The flare of his power surrounded them, warm with his scent. Heat threaded between her legs, but she was stronger than that. All she had to do was hold out for however long he took to say his piece.

He inhaled sharply, blew the breath out, and did it again. "This is hard. I've never told another person—any of this. I'm old. Very old."

She rolled her eyes. "So what. There's the odd one of us who lives past five or six hundred. I'm one of them."

Johannes shook his head. "Did you ever wonder where we came from? If we were a splinter group? A genetic aberration?" He stopped. "I'm stalling. I'm the first of us. Ceres made me as an experiment because of her love for animals."

Daria felt her eyes widen. Truth rode beneath his words. "But that must mean you're millennia old. How is that possible?"

He looked away and swallowed hard. "It's possible because I'm immortal."

"But none of the rest of us are."

"Ceres decided that part of her design was a mistake. She couldn't undo me, but she altered her template."

A rush of thoughts pummeled her, but one rose to the fore. "It's how you saved Max," she blurted. "You gave him your blood."

Johannes nodded, but didn't say anything.

"This is fascinating—and thanks for clearing up the mystery around Max—but why are you bothering to tell me any of this?"

He didn't meet her eyes, and his next words came with obvious effort. "I made a decision a very long time ago not to join my life to any woman's. Call me weak—or anything you want to—but the specter of watching someone I loved die wasn't a place I wanted to go. Especially not when it would happen over and over after I outlived everyone."

"I can see where that would be—"

"Let me finish," he said, his voice rough. "My cat believes you're my mated one. I suspect he's right because I've never felt such a strong attraction for anyone. If I'd been smarter—not so wiped out from the tension-laden trip in the hovercraft—I wouldn't have kissed you earlier."

"I knew you thought it was a mistake," she muttered, pain knifing through her as he corroborated her suspicions.

"Goddammit, Daria." He gripped her shoulders so hard pain shot down both arms. "It was only a mistake because I'm a weak, sorry son of a bitch. I was being selfish, thinking of how devastated I'd be after you died and I was alone—again. The mate bond is so pervasive, how could I live if I lost a mated one?"

"Others do." The hurt places inside her softened, and she wanted to close her arms around him, but held back.

"It doesn't excuse me, but other shifters might lose one mated one over the course of their lifetimes. They wouldn't have forever to process the depth of that loss. You understand the mate bond. It carves to the bottom of our hearts, our souls, our lives. Finding a mate is rare. It doesn't happen often."

When he raised his gaze, his eyes held a haunted look. "If I wasn't even strong enough to let myself fall in love with someone without the magic of the mate bond to bind us together..." His words trailed off, and he sounded so absolutely miserable, something inside her melted.

"We don't know we're mates. My cat thinks we are, but she's never given up hoping. I did long ago."

"You think you gave up." A bitter laugh bubbled out. "I stopped looking once the full impact of what *immortal* meant sank in. It's been a lonely life, but I came to terms with it. I broke a cardinal rule by telling you about myself. And by saving Max." His face twisted into a wry expression. "I've been expecting Ceres to drag me off and hurt me ever since I realized what my 'gift' to Max really meant. When I shared my blood with him, I had no idea it would make him immortal."

"Do you believe the gods still exist?"

"Why wouldn't they?"

It was a good question, and not one she had an answer for. "I don't know. Maybe because no one believes in them anymore, and they need some level of devotion to fuel their survival."

"I don't want to talk philosophy. I want to talk about us. I made a conscious choice I'd do anything I had to, including break my covenant with the goddess, if it meant getting you to listen to me. I didn't mean to hurt you earlier today."

He loosened his grip on her shoulders and cupped her face between his hands. "I care about you. Shit, you're all I can think about. Even when I was ferrying Max and Audrey all over hell, staying one step ahead of whoever wanted to blow us out of the skies, if I didn't watch it I saw your face, smelled your scent, and longed for you. Please, darling. Come back to my room. I want to make love with you."

"What if we don't shift? What if it turns out our cats are wrong, and we're not mated ones after all?"

"It doesn't matter. For once, I've made a decision that doesn't have me at its center. I want us to make a life together. If we're mates, so much the better. If not, I still want to try."

Reaching with tentative fingers, she stroked his face. The anguish in his eyes subsided, replaced by hope and hunger blazing in their depths.

"Let me take care of you, Daria. You'll never want for anything."

She smiled crookedly. "I don't want for much now."

"It's because you've set low standards." Her cat's acid tone was back in spades.

"I heard that." Johannes snickered. "I'm surprised my cat's held his tongue. Normally, silence isn't his long suit."

The feel of his skin beneath her fingers was electric, but she had things to say too. "I don't know about *low standards*," she murmured, "but I haven't been all that different from you. I've lived a long time, and when my mate never showed up, I decided it was easier to keep to myself."

"You wanted everything—or nothing." He wove his arms around her and trailed his fingertips down her back.

"Exactly. A few early experiments living with men I wasn't mated to convinced me that wasn't the answer. Besides, up until recently, I kept a very low profile. They hung witches and other women who practiced medicine out to dry."

"Forgive me for earlier?"

She nodded. "I was hurt, and I've done almost as good a job insulating myself from emotional pain as you."

The air glistened around them as he sheathed the barrier he'd constructed to keep their conversation private. "Will you come with me?"

Desire thickened her throat, and lust roared through her. Heat rose from her chest to her face, probably lending her a rosy tint. "I can't leave until Barney gets back."

"Of course not. How about if you ping his wrist computer?"

Almost as if he'd been standing outside the infirmary waiting, Barney strode through the door. He looked from her to Johannes and back again with his discerning, eagle-sharp gaze. "I've got it covered here, Sata."

She opened her mouth to thank him, but he waved her to silence and focused his next words at Johannes. "Remember the conversation we had in the garage?" At Johannes's nod, he continued. "If you do even one thing to make Daria unhappy—ever again—you will be one sorry bastard. Now go."

"Got it," Johannes replied. "I feel just as protective of her mental state as you."

"Thanks, Barney." Daria nodded his way.

"You don't have to thank me. Get moving."

She walked out of the infirmary with Johannes behind her. She knew what Barney's words had cost him, knew he loved her. He was a decent man, but there'd never been a spark on her side. At least she'd honored their friendship by being honest with him.

"He's a good man," Johannes murmured.

"The best. Which way?"

He held open a stairwell door. "Down one flight and then left. I'm in two-sixteen."

Her stomach fluttered, and her heart soared with hope. Had she finally found her mated one? What would the next hour yield? Would they shift while they made love?

"Thank you," her cat purred. *"Don't try to force it. Let it happen."*

Johannes joined her at the bottom of the stairs and threaded a hand around her waist. "Yeah, my cat is full of pithy advice too. I swear, I've never known the old guy to be so excited—about anything."

"How is it you can hear my cat?"

He shrugged and slapped his palm on a reader plate next to his door. "I don't know. It's part of my magic. I've always been able to hear other's bondmates to a greater or lesser degree." He stood aside for her to enter.

The door shut behind him with a tiny metallic *thunk* as the lock engaged. She turned to face him, and he held out his arms. "I'm nervous," he admitted. "Last thing I ever thought I'd feel with a beautiful woman so close."

"I'm nervous too," she said. "I want you so much it hurts, want you to be my mated one. I'm scared we'll make love, and nothing will happen."

"No matter what, something wonderful will happen." He smiled self-consciously, making him look young. "We'll pleasure each other. I'll get to worship your body. Bet it's better than my imagination."

"Flattery will get you everywhere." She walked into his arms and turned her face up, waiting for him to kiss her. Instead, he stroked her face and smoothed strands that had escaped from her braids aside. "You're so beautiful," he murmured. "I could look at you for hours, days, years, and never tire of the way light reflects off the planes of your face."

"You're the pretty one." She couldn't get any more words out. She wanted him with an intensity that stole her breath and tightened her throat.

He closed his mouth over hers. Unlike their kiss on the hovercraft landing pad, this one began softly. He brushed his lips over hers, stopped, and then did it again, almost as if he was giving her a choice.

She moved away slightly. "I want this. I want you."

Feral possessiveness lit his austere beauty. "Turn around."

"Why?"

"I'm going to unbraid your hair. I want to feel it surround me when I take you."

She felt him unravel her braids. Somewhere between running his hands through her loosened tresses, they found their way to her breasts. He strung kisses down one side of her neck as he tweaked her pebbled nipples. Groaning, alight with need that turned her insides molten, she turned in his arms.

This time, he crushed his lips over hers and plumbed her mouth with his tongue. She reached around him and grappled with his ass, drawing him as close as she could. The jut of his erection prodded her stomach, and Daria couldn't wait.

She had to see him, taste him, draw him inside her body. Wrenching away from his kiss, she tried to tell him what she needed, but gave up when the words stuck in her throat. Instead, she toed off her shoes and drew her top over her head. He surged toward her and pushed her bottoms down her legs, followed by her panties.

She closed her hand over the erection tenting the front of his pants and worked on undoing his zipper and the button holding his pants in place. While she did that, he tugged his blue cashmere sweater over his head and unbuttoned his long-sleeved shirt, shucking it. When she levered his trousers down his hips, he stepped out of them.

The only thing left was his shorts, and she pushed them out of the way. What little breath she had left escaped in a rush. Johannes naked was possibly the most perfect specimen she'd ever seen. Muscled shoulders and arms, a flat stomach, and strong legs. Everything perfectly proportioned, and skin a dusky, bronzy gold that looked as if it had been touched by fairy dust. His cock rose, thick and proud, from a mat of dark curls.

Because she couldn't stand not to touch it, she curled her fingers around him, and his erection jumped in her hand. He covered her breasts and teased the nipples to even harder points, before plunging a hand between her legs. The second he touched her clit, she dissolved into an orgasm. He rode it through with her, wringing the last drop of sensation from her spasming body.

Somehow, they were still on their feet. She herded him toward the bed. When he fell atop it, she followed him down, still hanging onto his cock. Threading kisses down his perfect chest, she closed her mouth around the head of his penis. He made a decidedly male sound and pushed deeper into her.

The world turned to lust. The air shimmered with sexual heat, and filled with his scent—male cat mixed with an amber under note that drove her wild. He pulled his cock from her mouth. She followed it, not done sucking on him, drinking him in, but he covered her waiting mouth with a hand.

"I love what you do to me, but I have to be inside you. Now. Turn over."

Daria understood. She wanted him inside her too. He'd kept rubbing her nub, and she was close to another release. She slithered around him and got to her hands and knees on the narrow bed. The head of his cock probed for entry, and she writhed under his touch. She'd never wanted a man inside her as much she wanted him.

Johannes sank into her, inch after glorious inch, until he'd filled her to the hilt. He twitched his wonderful penis, angling it just right, and she melted into another climax, heat rippling through her.

"We can get fancy later," he said, his voice so harsh with need, it was hard to understand him. "I can't wait."

He withdrew and drove himself into her, hard, sure, fast. His cock swelled, then swelled some more. Hot breath rasped against her back, and he closed his teeth over the junction of her neck and shoulder, biting hard. Pain—plus the spasms of his release as he shuddered inside her—shot her over the top again, and she came so hard the room spun around her.

From far away, she heard him crow. "We're shifting." Teeth bit again, and when she opened her lids, she saw through her cat's eyes.

She'd been so lost in rut, she'd stopped worrying about whether they'd shift or not. That they had was so miraculous, if she'd been human, she would've cried—just before she shrieked her victory to the skies.

His cock got even harder. Barbs scored her vulva, but she delighted in them. She hadn't had a mountain cat lover in centuries.

"Told you," her cat screeched and raked its claws down the bedclothes, shredding them. *"Told you."*

CHAPTER 8

Johannes dove into his cat's consciousness. He'd doubted his animal's assessment of Daria because finding his mated one felt like a pipedream. He'd never been so glad to be wrong about something. His cat's joy spilled through him as it fucked Daria's cat. What a gorgeous animal she was. Her pelt was dark brown with golden highlights that made it gleam like hammered bronze. He couldn't see her eyes, but he imagined they'd be clear amber, or maybe even green.

Desire cut through him, so clean and pure every other sexual experience in his life paled by comparison. His cat cock swelled, barbs catching on the folds inside Daria's scorching heat. Semen pumped out of him. Cat sex was different. He'd keep right on feeding jism into her until his balls were dry.

Beneath him, she arched her back and yowled as her body contracted around him. He bit her other shoulder for good measure, thrilled when she tightened her sheath still more around his shuddering cock. Pleasure gradually faded, replaced by a glow that warmed him from his head to his tail tip to his paws.

His cat was lost in post-coital bliss, too sated to say a word. As his penis gradually softened, he pulled from the warmth of her body. She spun to face him, lithe and light on her feet.

"I wanted to see what you look like as a cat. Peeking over my shoulder didn't quite yield the whole picture."

He batted her with a playful paw. *"Well? Here I am."*

"You're gorgeous. I thought your pelt would be darker, but it's almost golden. Your eyes are the same dynamite green."

"And yours are blue. I'd never have guessed. So beautiful." He swiped his tongue over her snout, and she licked him in return.

"I wish we could go outside and run together."

"Someday, darling. It's not safe here."

"I know." The air around her took on a glistening, liquid aspect, and her human body took form.

Johannes shifted too. He felt different, somehow. Savage protectiveness surged, and he understood how much energy he'd poured into pretending that finding a mate wasn't important. "We'll get Max to perform the mating ceremony just as soon as we can."

"Are you certain you don't want to make it through the next few days? I could get nailed by enemy fire, and then you'd be mated to a dead woman, just like in your worst imaginings."

He started to tell her the first thing they were going to do was see she got an infusion of his blood, but stopped. What he'd done with Max was excusable—barely—since he hadn't known. Now that he did know, creating more immortal shifters truly shit all over his covenant with Ceres.

"I know what you're thinking," she said softly and put her arms around him, cradling him against the curves of her body. "Now that the mate bond is alive between us, I can see into your mind."

He waited, gave her a chance to say more, before asking, "Do you want me to—?"

Daria shook her head. "I don't want to offer Ceres any reason to take you away from me. I'm so happy right now. Everything is perfect. I can't believe I finally found my mated one. Fate wouldn't be cruel enough to sweep all that joy out from under us." She pirouetted out of his arms and floated around the room, happiness sheeting from her in iridescent waves.

Her body was a study in poetry. Broad, muscled shoulders, small breasts tipped with copper nipples, a slender waist and slightly flared hips. Her legs were long and shapely, and her unbound hair brushed her ass.

"You move like a dancer."

"Close." She sent a grin his way. "Black belt Aikido."

"But you have your cat if you need to fight."

Her smile dimmed a notch. "Not always. Sometimes shifting isn't a good idea." She made her way into his arms, hugging him close. "You've made me very happy. I'm falling head over heels over tail and, it's the most amazing feeling."

Johannes returned her embrace. It was amazing. All the new feelings cascading through him filled him with delight.

A staunch knock on his door startled him, and he sent magic scuttling through it to see who was there. His chest tightened. Max was on the other side.

"Is our honeymoon over already?" Daria asked.

"Probably." He grabbed two robes out of the closet and tossed one her way. Once they were both covered, he tugged his door open. "Thank God you didn't show up fifteen minutes earlier," he growled, doing his damnedest to sound annoyed, but nothing could destroy his good mood. "What's happened now?"

Max muscled his way inside, inhaling deeply. "I got reports of caterwauling from everyone in this sector. Thought I'd check things out for myself." He smiled, looking pleased. "Smells like mated sex to me." He reached into a pocket and brandished a ritual mating stone. "Thought you might need me to officiate."

The door that hadn't fully closed swooshed open. Audrey, Devon, Kate, and Ryan crowded into the room.

"It's true," Kate announced after snuffling noisily. "We have another newly mated pair." Applause and cheers broke out.

"How can you tell?" Audrey asked.

"Breathe deep," Kate advised her. "Nothing has quite the satisfied stench of mated sex."

Daria started to laugh. "Will I ever have another private moment?"

"Probably not," Johannes replied. "What about Max's offer? Would you like him to join us?"

She trained her liquid, dark gaze on him. "Would you?"

Johannes nodded. "Yes. You're already my mate in spirit. We should solemnize our bond with the ancient ritual."

More shifters crowded through the open doorway.

"Maybe we should move this to the computer room," Max murmured. "Things have been so grim around here, having a wedding will surely rally everyone's spirits."

"We can have the human part," Daria spoke up, "but for the animal coupling, I'd like that to be a little more private."

"Of course, of course," Max agreed. He glanced at his wrist computer. "How about if we meet in one hour. That will give me time to let everyone know and for us to whip up some special food."

"Sounds great, but all I have to wear are scrubs," Daria said.

"I'll find you something," Kate volunteered. "There are clothing lockers here. It won't be fancy, but I'll bet we can find you a skirt or a dress."

Johannes shook his head to dispel disbelief. Today had morphed from one of the hardest days of his life to one of the most special in the blink of an eye. He still couldn't quite believe it.

"You did great," his cat offered. *"Not sure when you stopped trusting my instincts, but—"*

"No lectures. Not today."

A deep, throaty purr followed. *"No lectures. Just hurry up and get to the second part of the ritual so I can fuck Daria's cat again. She's one hot, juicy number. Come on. Hurry! Chop. Chop."*

Laughter bubbled out of Johannes. His cat had always been forthright and robust, not shy about calling a spade a spade, but his current enthusiasm level was off the charts.

Max clapped his hands together. "Come on, people. Move it! We have a ceremony to plan."

Everyone shuffled out to the accompaniment of excited murmurs and shouted congratulations.

"Come with me." Kate grabbed Daria's arm. "Let's see if we can turn you into a bride."

"Do not change one thing about her," Johannes snarled, practically choking on possessiveness. "I love her just like she is."

Kate nudged Daria. "Don't you just adore it when they go all Neanderthal?"

Daria laughed. "I have no idea. Let's stop by the infirmary. I want to make sure Barney knows. Maybe we can come up with someone else to watch over my patients, so he can come to the ceremony."

"You got it, hon." Kate herded Daria out of the room.

Johannes gazed around the small space. It still smelled of Daria, and the remembered feel of her in his arms and around his sensitive ridged flesh spawned another erection. His newly hard cock curved against his belly, hungry for more.

"Go get her," his cat urged. *"Bring her back to us. Now."*

"She wants to look beautiful for the mating ceremony."

"Pfft." A hissing yowl. *"She's already beautiful, and you're already mated. Never did understand all the rest of it when the other bond animals described the cuts and marks with the stone."*

"Maybe you'll understand more once we've lived it."

"Not likely." His cat subsided amid a flurry of whuffly snarls.

Johannes picked up the clothing he'd taken off. Maybe it would do, along with a fresher shirt. He caught a peek of his reflection in the wall-mounted mirror and saw he was grinning like a love-besotted fool.

He mock jabbed a right hook at the mirror and then felt silly. He'd never been this full of joy—ever. By all the gods, he hoped to hell they'd get to the other side of the confrontation Max planned fast.

Yeah, and it damn sure better have a good outcome.

He wanted to take his mate and retire from the world for a while. Certainly, for long enough to raise their first few children. Johannes made a grab for his out-of-control thoughts. That was what he wanted, but Daria might see things differently. He'd underwrite however she wanted to do things…

Maybe.

If I can.

She needed to slow down and take things easier. He never wanted to see gray circles under her eyes again, or have her be so exhausted she passed out in her hovercraft.

Easy. Slow down. We'll work everything out together.

Tightening the belt of his robe, he strode out his door intent on a shower at the community bathroom a couple of doors down the hall.

~

Daria smoothed a black jersey skirt over her hips and adjusted the shimmery teal sweater over it. Kate fussed with her hair, brushing it until it shone with blue highlights.

"There." The other woman stepped back and cast a critical eye over her work. "You're ravishing."

"Thank you. I didn't really need all this, but it's lovely just the same."

"You're right." Kate nodded. "It's just window-dressing. Devon and I were dressed in borrowed sweats when Max joined us, and we didn't get to the animals' role until several days had passed. Devon was wounded, and he had to heal enough a shift wouldn't rip his stitches out. It didn't help matters that Audrey and I were kidnapped and—"

"Kidnapped? Part of the mess we're dealing with now?"

"Yeah." Kate inhaled sharply. "Splinter groups nabbed us, but Max talked sense into most of them."

Daria glanced at her wrist computer. They still had a few

minutes. "I want to hear the rest of that story sometime, but for now I'm more interested in the mate bond. Did your life change much?"

Kate settled into a chair across from where Daria sat. They were in one of many small, empty meeting rooms in the underground facility. "You're scared."

"Maybe not scared, but it's a big change. I've been by myself for a long time." She paused a beat. "You didn't exactly answer me."

"No. I didn't." Kate drew her red brows together. "Of course my life changed, but the mate bond smooths out the rough spots. I totally quit working—"

"Really? Why? Is that one of the rules? If so, I haven't heard it before." Daria cut in, certain she'd keep right on doctoring until Death pulled the scalpel from her hand.

"Whoa!" Kate held up a hand, laughing. "I worked as a surrogate. Couldn't very well keep on teaching men about the joys of sex. Devon would've killed every single one of them."

Daria grinned. "Yeah, guess I can see where that might've been a problem. I've sent a few humans to surrogates. Never a shifter, though."

"No reason to. We do pretty well in the sex department, even when we're not mated. Back to your question." Kate's expression grew serious. "Of course there will be changes, but the mate bond is worth every single one of them. It will enrich your life—Johannes's too—beyond anything you've ever imagined."

"Thanks for the pep talk." Daria snorted. "I needed it. Bride's jitters and all, but this is probably a good place to stop. We should get moving. Don't want to be late for my own mating ceremony."

A gentle tap on the door was followed by Barney opening it. "Wanted to get a peek at you before you gave yourself away."

Daria got to her feet and opened her arms. Barney hugged her. "Happy for you, Sata. Truly I am, even though I'll never find a mate—"

"And why not?" Kate demanded.

Barney stepped away from Daria. "Because I'm an eagle. There's no one to mate with. There are limits to cross species mate bonds. And all the other eagles left are first degree relatives."

"There aren't many of you." Kate spoke slowly. "But I've met a few."

"Likely all first line relatives." He repeated and rolled his eyes. "It's okay. I accepted it a long time ago. See both you gals at the ceremony." He turned and trotted out the door.

"We've got a couple of eagles here," Kate murmured. "They're new arrivals from New Zealand. Maybe..."

"Have you always been a matchmaker?" Daria walked through the door and headed for the computer room.

"It's always been a side interest. I've been lots of things, but most of them have involved teaching someone something. How about you? Always mucked around with healing?"

"Yup. That's me." Daria turned down a stairwell. "The original mucker."

The computer room's door had been propped open. She walked through and saw Johannes at the far end of the room. He'd obviously been waiting for her because his face broke into a broad grin when they made eye contact. Damn, but he looked good. His dark brown hair gleamed with golden highlights, and he'd left it loose to trail past his shoulders. He wore black slacks and the pale blue sweater from earlier, but with a silky dark shirt beneath it.

A warm tide of emotion started in her toes and swept through her, making everything tingle with anticipation. This was the real deal. The mating ceremony. Something she'd watched plenty of times—and been certain she'd never participate in.

"Aren't you glad you listened to me?" Her cat was close to the surface, champing at the bit to couple with Johannes's cat again.

"Yes, sweetie, very glad."

Johannes held out both hands. When she got close, she gripped them and felt his energy pour into her, igniting all her nerve endings with love and longing.

"Look at everything our people did for us," he murmured.

She'd had eyes only for him, but she cast her gaze over the room. It was lovely. Tables with food and drink lined one wall, and someone had fashioned crepe paper flowers along the ceiling and walls. "It's beautiful," she agreed, "but not surprising. Shifters love sex first and parties second."

"What an incorrigible lot we are." Humor gleamed behind his eyes.

Max swept toward them, dressed in a gray suit, white shirt, and blue tie. "Ready?"

When she repeated the question internally, Daria realized she'd been ready to find a mate forever. When it hadn't happened, she'd pushed her loneliness aside, burying it deep where it couldn't haunt her.

No more.

"More than ready." She tilted her chin up.

"Me too." Johannes positioned himself by her side.

Hold out your right hands." Max made two quick strokes along the meaty place beneath their thumbs. "Place the cuts together until your blood mingles. Hold them there and repeat after me. *Body of my body, blood of my blood, now and forever more, I shall be yours.*"

Daria spoke the words.

Johannes's green eyes glowed with love, lending an ethereal aspect to his striking good looks. Then it was his turn, and he repeated the same chant.

Daria's cat did flip-flops inside her, right along with her heart. Johannes was really and truly hers, now and forever. Joy swelled within her. Johannes made it even more perfect by bending his head and kissing her.

Max smiled like a beneficent father. "Best part of being an elected leader," he murmured. "Wish I got to do this more often." He wrapped linen cloths around their wounds, and Daria made certain they soaked up all the blood.

Johannes unwound the linen. "I'll keep these, and we can bury them in a safe place."

Hoots, whistles, and cheers rose around them.

"Dig in, everyone," Max shouted over the din of the crowd. "The newly mated pair and I will be right back."

"*Finally*," Daria's cat yowled, and a flash of sexual heat rolled through her, turning her insides molten.

Johannes threaded an arm around her waist. "We'll be right behind you," he told Max.

"Better hurry," Daria murmured. "If we don't, my cat will break loose, and all my borrowed finery will end up in shreds."

Max picked up his pace, and they loped from the room. A few shifters threw ribald suggestions after them, which made Daria's cat even harder to control. She wanted Johannes's cat again, and she wanted him now.

One floor up, Max came to such a precipitous halt they ran into his back. He rested his palm on the reader, and a black door swung open.

"You're letting us use the growing room?" Johannes's question was cloaked in incredulity.

"Unless you'd rather be elsewhere." Max turned to face them. "I thought this would get you closer to our roots in the outdoors than any of the rest of this place."

"Not at all. It's wonderful. If you'd given me a choice, it's what I'd have chosen." Johannes nudged her. "Max must really like you."

"Well, she helped keep me alive after your sleight of hand." Max's blue eyes twinkled.

Daria gazed at the large room filled with hydroponic grow boxes, hosing, and the delicious smell of growing vegetables. "It's perfect." She eyed the complex maze of walkways between the boxes. An ideal place for two cats to chase each another.

"*Hurry*," her cat screeched. "*Hurry*." Waves roiled through Daria, prodding her to shift.

"I'll wait outside for a few minutes," Max told them. "By then you'll have found your cats."

She didn't wait to watch him leave. Kicking off her shoes, she dragged her top over her head and slithered out of her skirt. Next to her, Johannes shucked his clothes. The second she was naked, her cat blasted into her. She'd never shifted so fast. Johannes wasn't quite there yet, so she took off at a run.

"Catch me." She threw down the gauntlet, challenging him.

Paws pounded behind her. She ducked under a long grow box and switched direction, tail twitching with the thrill of luring him into a tight corner where she could pounce. Too bad she didn't have a dick. She'd love to be on top, pouring heat into him.

Teeth closed over her tail, but she tugged free and kept running. Gods, it felt good to let her cat form be free. One of the big drawbacks to her killer work schedule was she hadn't shifted for more than a few moments in months.

A flash of movement caught her eye, and then Johannes vaulted atop her back. He closed his teeth over the ritual biting spot on her neck, and she felt his cock slam home. It was almost too big to get inside. Cat sex usually began with the male only partially hard, but running after her had apparently gotten Johannes fiercely excited.

She wound her tail off to one side and arched her back to give him deep access to the secrets of her body. Her cat purred, yowled, and screeched as sexual hunger tinged with the wonder of finding their one, true mate shot through them.

As soon as his cock was seated, Johannes began pumping jism into her. Somewhere in the midst of all that heat and the alluring scent of musky male cat, fire scored her sides. Hissing in annoyance, she twisted her head and saw Max bent over them, ritual stone in hand, marking them while they mated.

He made certain their blood mingled before discreetly vanishing from sight.

Johannes bit harder, and his cock swelled even bigger inside her. Pleasure rocked her as she rode from the crest of one surge to the next, abandoning the old wave when the new one carried her to a new crescendo.

Time stopped. They could've coupled for minutes or hours. She truly didn't know. It was one of the good things about being in her cat's body. Things like time didn't matter.

Finally, Johannes's cock softened and slithered from her body. She reached for her human form because she wanted to wrap her arms around him and lay her lips atop his. He must've read the same script because, human again, he drew her against his nakedness, murmuring endearments in the eldritch shifter tongue. She'd known it once, but had let it slide out of memory.

"I love you, Daria. You've made me a very happy man."

Because words were beyond her, she snuggled closer, hoping he could feel her love in the touch of her hands on his hard-muscled flesh.

"I'd rather spirit you away and make love until we can't anymore, but we should spend time with the well-wishers," he said. "If we wait too long, there won't be any food left, and they'll all have gone to bed."

She pulled away and looked up at him. "I'd like to close out the world forever, but you're right." Rising on tiptoes, she kissed him gently and went to hunt down their clothes.

It was important to share their joy with the shifters in the computer room one floor down. Mate bonds had become rare, and believing in shifter magic might give her kin hope to carry them through the next span of days.

She handed Johannes his clothing and dressed quickly.

He laid a hand on her arm. "Before we go, I need to ask you something."

"What?" She cocked her head to one side. He looked uncomfortable.

"Are you planning to come with us when we go back to Sacramento?"

"Huh? I didn't know we were going back there. At least not anytime soon."

"That's right. I didn't tell you. Max has a plan."

"From what I know about Max, he always has a plan. Spill it, mated one. Even before I hear what it is, the answer to your question is this. Wherever you go, I'll be by your side."

"Not going to let me keep you sequestered and safe?" His sensuous mouth twisted into a smile.

"Not on your life. Sketch out the high points of Max's brainchild, and then we'll join the party."

CHAPTER 9

Though he and Daria carved out time here and there, the remainder of the week flew by. Thank Christ there hadn't been any further attacks on their people. The infirmary had cleared out except for a few severely wounded—and even they were progressing nicely. Shifters healed fast, which was a good thing.

Johannes spent long hours in meetings with Max, Ryan, and Devon, honing their plan to something close to perfection. They couldn't predict all the variables, but they did have one primary attack plan, plus three fallback ones. Somehow, it was midday Thursday, and they'd gathered for a final powwow before making their way back to Sacramento via a variety of what they hoped would be near-invisible transportation.

The two tech experts sitting in on the discussions exchanged glances. "Did you get us the schematics for the capitol's vid feed?" one asked. A coyote shifter, he was tall and rangy, with silver hair and intense blue eyes.

Max frowned. "Abe, right?" At the man's nod, Max went on, "Thanks for the reminder. I'd ordered them up. Let me go check to see if they ever showed."

"Good, because—"

A knock on the conference room door scattered Johannes's concentration. He didn't need magic to tell him Daria was in the hall. Her energy burned bright, drawing him like a beacon.

"I'll let her in," Devon said. "I'm closest to the door."

"Nah, I'll get it." Max sprang to his feet. "I need to find those schematics for Abe."

"If they're not there," Josh—the other tech guy—spoke up, "we'll be flying blind."

"You'll get what you need." Max sounded fierce. "If I have to hack into the capitol's database myself." He opened the door, greeted Daria, and disappeared.

"Sorry to interrupt." She moved into the room and made her way to Johannes's side. "I just got a call from dispatch. There's been another attack. Smaller this time, but they asked for me."

Johannes chewed his lip, not liking her going where he couldn't protect her. "Where?"

"Down by the Mexican border."

"Can you stall them?"

Emotion played across her face. Sorrow for their people under attack. Guilt for not being able to save everyone. "Not easily."

"How about this?" Ryan spoke up. "It's not safe for us to travel right now, and that's a long way. Maybe they can find people closer to the event."

"Good point." Johannes thought about it, and understanding surfaced. They called Daria because she never said no. Her total devotion to healing was probably legendary.

She laid a hand on his shoulder. "Watch those thoughts. But guilty as charged. I hardly ever say no."

"This time you will," Johannes muttered. It was one thing dragging her into danger when he was by her side. Quite another if he was six hundred miles away.

"It's what I thought, but I wanted to check in with all of you." A grim expression settled her honed Asian features into a harsh mask.

"I figure I'll be plenty busy once we barricade ourselves into the capitol."

"Jesus, I hope not." Abe's lean face twisted into a grimace. "I'm much comfier with circuit boards and tools than with guns."

"See you in a few." Daria bent and laid her cheek against Johannes's before heading for the door.

"What will you tell them?" Johannes asked.

"That I have patients here who aren't out of the woods yet. And that I'm worried about traveling with so much political unrest." She paused to take a breath. "I have our things together. Whenever you want to get moving, I'm ready."

He watched her leave. Longing filled him so full he almost couldn't breathe. He finally, finally had a mate, but he couldn't do all the things he'd assumed would happen if he ever got that lucky. No extended trips wandering through Greek ruins or yachting in the Caribbean. No retreat to the mansion he still maintained in northern Greece. Shock ran through him when he realized he hadn't even visited the place in over a hundred years. It might not still be standing, for all he knew. He'd shielded it with magic, but his wards had likely dissipated, given all the time that had passed.

"Hey, boss." Ryan waved a hand in front of Johannes's face.

"Huh? Oh, sorry." He inhaled deep and blew it out. "We were pretty much done here, weren't we?"

"Yeah," Devon muttered. "I'm going to run Kate down, and then we'll start driving."

"We'll do the same once we hear from Max," Abe said. "I'm pretty sure he said Ryan would be with us."

"I will be," Ryan confirmed. "In fact, I'm driving. You guys can take advantage of the time to firm up your attack plan."

"Sounds good to me," Abe said.

The door clicked open and Max trotted in. All smiles, he clicked keys on his wrist computer. One of the screens lining the room flared to life. "There," he announced. "You can download what you need from the vid feed."

Josh and Abe surged toward the screen, studying it. "Excellent." Abe gave a thumbs-up sign.

"Indeed." Josh, another coyote who could've been an Abe clone, agreed. "Very straightforward." He pointed to several electronic hubs. "Whoever designed this didn't do it to protect data flow. We can set up jams to keep things open here, here, here, and there."

"How long can you hold them?" Max asked.

"Several hours," Abe said.

"Whatever you can do, we'll make sure it's enough," Johannes spoke up. He got to his feet. "I'm out of here. See all of you at our appointed places."

"Sure you don't want to fly?" Max asked.

Johannes made a grunting noise. "Last place I want to be again is in a hovercraft. No thank you. I'm sure I'll get over it, but Daria and I will drive. If we need to, we'll find a cash only motel, but I'd rather drive straight through, so we'll be in position sometime later tonight. I'm sure there will be a million odds and ends to take care of."

"Good enough." Max said.

"Are you certain they'll let you back inside the capitol?" Johannes narrowed his eyes. "I've been checking the news, and it doesn't appear you've been made, but that means the ones who targeted my hovercraft—because they were certain you were in it—are keeping a very low profile."

"It's one of the things we don't know," Devon said. "I've been watching the news like a hawk. And I've had Kate monitoring every single channel—even the sub-rosa ones."

Max eyed Devon. "I know you were planning to drive, but how about if you and Kate fly with us?"

"Sure." Devon nodded. "We can do that. Probably good to have extra weapons at the ready to protect you."

Max straightened his shoulders, standing tall. "I raised Loren on his secure channel."

"And?" Johannes held his breath. Loren was the head of Max's security detail at the capitol.

"He was delighted I was safe." Max paused. "He couldn't fake that level of relief, and he agreed to meet me on the roof later tonight."

"Did you ask him…anything?" Ryan asked.

"Tried to. He said he'd talk with me when he saw me."

"Interesting," Johannes growled. "Means he knows something."

"Yeah," Max agreed. "Something that will help us. Now go. This will play out just fine. Have faith."

"Spoken like a politician." Johannes snorted laughter.

"You know what they say," Max replied.

"They say lots of things," Johannes countered. "Right now I'm thinking about the power corrupts deal."

"If I ever get to a point where I have absolute power—" Max looked sidelong at him "—be sure to let me know if it's corrupted me absolutely."

"Good note to leave on." Johannes slugged him in the shoulder as he loped out of the room, intent on finding Daria to see how her conversation with medical dispatch had gone. He hoped to hell they hadn't guilt-tripped her into agreeing. He didn't know quite what he'd do if that were the case.

He made his way to their room. Daria wasn't there, so he headed for the infirmary and found her and Barney deep in conversation.

"…need to take me with you," Barney was saying.

Johannes stopped inside the doorway. He hadn't even considered Daria's medical sidekick.

She trained her dark gaze on him. "You heard the tail end of that. What do you think?"

"How much do you know?" Johannes asked the other man.

"Only that Daria is going somewhere with you, and that she's worried enough about it, she turned down dispatch's latest assignment." He moved closer to Johannes. "Daria never, never tells dispatch no. I figured if she did, it means she's going somewhere she'll be doctoring. If that's true, she'll need me."

"What do you think?" Johannes addressed the question to Daria.

"Barney has a point. There are many procedures I can't do without another shifter to help me."

"It's dangerous," Johannes said. "And you can't tell anyone."

"Everything Daria and I do is at least potentially dangerous," Barney countered. "And it's hard to tell anyone shit, since I have no idea where we're headed."

"Okay," Johannes said. "I'll let Max know we'll have one more." He tapped a few keys on his wrist computer.

"See you in our room," Daria said. "I need to write out instructions for the patients here. Anyone can see to them at this point. And I need to fill Barney in on at least a few things, so he can decide if this is what he truly wants to do."

"I'll tell Max that too, so he can assign someone to infirmary duty." Johannes bent to kiss Daria before leaving the room. His head was stuffed full of last minute arrangements, and he wanted to make certain he'd have everything they needed. If Max's plan worked—and he was convinced it had at least a fifty-fifty chance—he'd be able to spirit Daria away soon.

The thought of hours, days, weeks, and months romping by her side in both their human and cat forms, making love whenever they wanted, and just enjoying one another filled him with unbearable longing. To counteract the erection pushing uncomfortably against his tight Levis, he headed for the munitions room to restock his ammunition. Nothing like thinking about an assault rifle to kill sexual yearning.

Daria let herself into the room she shared with Johannes. They'd moved a second cot into it and pushed them together to create a big enough space for them to sleep comfortably. Not that they'd done a hell of a lot of sleeping. In truth, they'd fucked so much she was sore, but it was a sweet ache that reminded her how much she wanted him. Almost as if he'd been inside her head—and he spent almost as much time harvesting her thoughts as he did inside the rest of her body—Johannes strolled through the door.

His face lit when he saw her. "What a delightful surprise." He dropped a paper sack full of something that clanked metallically in a corner.

"For me too." She melted into his arms, letting his clean, fresh scent surround her. "Mmm, you always smell so good."

"So do you." He threaded his hands into the tangle of her braids. Once her head was cradled between his hands, he licked her mouth, teased it with little biting motions until she opened to his caress, and he plunged his tongue inside.

She sucked hungrily on it wishing it was his cock. Amusement flared. She never thought she'd have a love affair with a man's penis, but she adored Johannes's. It was almost impossible to keep her hands off him when they were alone together. As if it was tuned in to her thoughts, the part of his anatomy she'd been fixating on swelled against her belly.

Reluctantly, she broke their kiss. "Do we have time?"

"Probably not, but why should we let that stop us?"

Daria laughed. God, it felt good to laugh with Johannes. Delight spilled through her, reminding her of something besides Death stalking them on all sides. She reached for his belt and undid it. Next, her eager fingers fumbled with his pants.

"You forgot my shoes, darling." He grinned down at her.

"I never *forget* anything," she informed him loftily, but it was a tough charade to pull off when she was so hot all she wanted was him inside her. As fast as possible. "I had something else in mind."

Dropping to her knees, she extracted his more-than-hard-on from the confines of pants and shorts and sank the smooth, velvety tip into her mouth.

He groaned and placed his hands on either side of her head, guiding her efforts. "I love the heat of your mouth on me," he told her. "The scrape of your teeth, the way you suckle me and move your hands on my shaft. Harder, darling. Do it harder. You won't hurt me."

His cock bucked in her hands. She moved her mouth from him long enough to say, "Talk dirty to me. Tell me what you want to do to me." She rubbed her thighs together, the friction against her swollen clit almost enough to make her come.

He pressed his cock back between her lips, and she tasted the salt tang of liquid dribbling from him when he got excited. "I want to run my tongue over every inch of you. I love the way your nipples get long and hard when I suck on them, and the way your clit grows when I tease it. Your beautiful golden skin turns this amazing tawny rose shade. Remember last night when I started with your toes sucking them, and you came before I even made it to your knees?"

She did remember, and the image made her frantic with lust. Moving one of her hands from him, she slipped it between her legs and rubbed herself over her clothes.

The tempo of Johannes thrusting increased, along with his breathing. She dragged her mouth from him and licked up his belly to his nipples. When she flicked them with her tongue, he made a low, guttural sound. It was full of fire and possessiveness, and she wanted him desperately.

"How it is you still have your clothes on?" His words were so thick it was hard to understand him. He tugged her top over her head and pushed her pants down, but her legs tangled in them.

Daria twisted in his arms and sucked his erection again, but he pulled from her mouth. "Clothes off," he demanded. "All of them. Mine too."

He bent to unlace his shoes and toed them off. She did the same. Once that was done, the rest of their clothes flew around the room. She wasn't sure who took what off, but the net result was both of them naked and panting. His nipples were hard buds, and his cock curved against his belly.

"How do you want us to be?" he asked.

So crazed with wanting him, it almost didn't matter, she lay on her back and drew her knees up. He hurtled between her thighs and slammed his cock to the hilt. He liked to watch her while they made love. At first his intense green gaze made her uncomfortable, self-conscious, but she'd come to appreciate losing herself in the wonder of his eyes.

Daria tightened her legs around his waist and hung on while he fucked her with debauched abandon. The climax that began brewing the second he walked into their room boiled out of her, and she convulsed around him. He'd ride it through. He loved to feel her come, to watch passion play itself out across her face and body. He'd told her so enough times.

"You are unbelievably gorgeous," he rasped. "I still can't believe you're mine."

Daria could relate because the same sense of disbelief coursed through her. "You're the most beautiful man in the world, in the universe. I can't believe you're mine, let alone my mated one."

"Believe it."

He let himself down atop her, moved his hands beneath her buttocks, and flipped them so she was on top. "Straddle me. I want to watch your breasts bounce while you fuck me."

Happy to give her mate anything he wanted, she stabilized herself on her knees and let him set a rhythm for them. When he moved a hand to inscribe teasing circles around her clit, she gave herself up to sensation sheeting through her.

"Now!"

His voice surrounded her, part mental, part out loud, and her body slid into another climax. He joined her, the spasms of his release rocketing her into yet a third orgasm. They clung to each other for long moments, savoring the intensity of their binding, while their breathing returned to normal.

She relaxed into his embrace, and he stroked hair back from her sweaty face. "Do you have stuff together for us?" he asked.

"I have my medical supplies, or Barney does. Beyond that, we didn't bring much with us when we came here."

"I need my computer equipment and guns. The rest doesn't matter." He kissed her forehead and slid from under her body.

"Guess that means we need to get moving." She hated to leave the room where she and Johannes had first made love.

"'Fraid so." He kissed her again, then wiped himself off with a towel and sorted his clothes from the tangle on the floor.

Something he'd said sank in, and she joined him, taking the towel to dry herself before she dressed. "Guns."

"Yes, guns." He flashed her a smile worthy of Ares, God of War. "I never go anywhere without them."

"The things a girl finds out about her mate." She tried to joke, but he saw through her.

"Daria. You don't have to do this. You can stay here. I'll come back for you once it's over." Johannes stood before her, pleading in his eyes. It was obviously what he wanted her to do.

"We started out as equals. I'm not going to hide behind you and let you fight my battles for me. Shifter freedom is just as important to me as it is to you, and I wouldn't feel very good about myself if I laid low just because I'm scared."

"And that, my dearest love, is why I'm not forcing you to remain behind. Because I love and respect you too much not to accede to your wishes. Ready?"

She nodded.

"I will be. Give me a few." He pushed the small closet open and extracted his duffels and a bag holding an assault rifle. A quick check yielded ammunition, two other guns, and computer accoutrements. He made a grab for the paper sack he'd carted into the room and added racks of ammunition to his rifle bag.

"I guess all that was always in our closet." An uncomfortable laugh found its way out.

Johannes couldn't die. She could, and they were heading into a direct confrontation with people who wanted every single shifter deader than dirt. She cared a whole lot more about staying alive now that she was mated than she ever had before, and it made her vulnerable—and nervous.

I can't think that way.

Have to stay positive.

Apparently oblivious to her inner turmoil, Johannes winked at her. "Yup. Pays to check up on us shifter dudes. You never know what twisted places—"

She swatted him. "Let's get moving. We're probably late."

"We are." He cupped the side of her face. "But it was worth every minute." Drawing away, he asked. "Do you know how to fire a gun?"

"Yeah. Not real good at it, but I've done a little target practice."

"Here." He drew a lethal looking old-style pistol out of the suitcase, popped a clip into it, and handed it to her. "This is the safety—"

"I know that much." Wordlessly, she dropped it into her bag, hoping to hell she wouldn't have to use it. She was sworn to protect life, not take it. "Why not a laser pistol?"

"Because that Smith and Wesson .45 has a hell of a lot better stopping power."

He shut his case and snapped it up. She shouldered her bag. When he held their door open for her, she walked through it.

"Where are we meeting Barney?" Johannes asked. "Or are we?"

"We are. He'll be in the garage. I told him enough for him to make a decision, but not everything."

She hunted for a place to shelve her fear. This was a lot like medical triage in a war zone. If she could focus on what was in front of her—not get too far ahead of the curve—she'd get through it.

CHAPTER 10

Johannes pulled off at a recharging station to the side of the interstate. It was closing on midnight, and so far, so good. They were only about twenty miles from Sacramento, and they'd had a free ride, at least so far.

"Seems like this is going exceedingly well," Daria murmured.

"Yeah, too well," Barney grumbled from the backseat.

"Ever the pessimist," Daria tossed over one shoulder.

"One of us needs to be grounded in reality. Open your door, Sata. I'm going outside to pee."

"Good idea." Daria got out, and then followed him to the collection of stinking Sani-cans lined up at the end of the charging station. Water was too valuable to waste on flush toilets.

Johannes took advantage of not being behind the wheel to bend over his wrist computer. He wanted to check in with Max on the secure frequency they'd hammered out.

Daria walked to his side and waited until he was done. "Well?" She raised an inquisitive brow.

"He and Audrey and Kate and Devon are in position in his office. Josh and Abe beat them there, and Max has already begun his message to the people through the vid feed."

"You look relieved."

Johannes nodded. "I am. Four of them traveling together in a hovercraft was risky, but having all of us strung out along the interstate wasn't much better. It's good Ryan got the tech dudes in place."

"So we'll be the last ones," Daria said. "Has Max heard anything from the other shifter cadres you told me would show up in Sacramento tomorrow morning?"

"No, but we didn't expect to. Radio silence is always safest before a coup."

Daria frowned. "But you just called Max."

"Yeah, and I kept it to ninety seconds. Too short to trace."

"You hope." Barney joined them. He glanced at the charger. "Looks like we have at least half an hour here." He shook his head. "I heard most of that. If Max has started transmitting, it's only a matter of time before SWAT teams converge on the capitol to try to shut him up."

"Probably true, but we won't be here that long," Johannes replied. "We don't need a full charge. We actually had enough juice to make it—unless we hit an unexpected traffic jam. I didn't want to take chances so close to our goal."

"Probably wise." Barney elbowed Daria. "Did you turn off your chip?"

"No. Thanks for the reminder." She pushed on the webbing between her fourth and fifth fingers, waited, and then did it again. "Check me," she told Barney, "and then I'll do the same for you."

"What are the two of you doing?" Johannes asked.

"Dispatch has ways of finding us. It's to ensure they can extract us from difficult situations," Daria explained. "If they can't raise us on our wrist computers."

"What? They embed microchip transmitters?"

"Yup." Barney flashed an electronic transponder over Daria. It beeped several times. "You're clean. Now do me."

She took the item from him, and repeated his actions. The

device looked like an old-fashioned cell phone, with a flashing display. "You're clean too. Good you remembered."

He smiled sheepishly. "Probably because I turn mine off from time to time. Whenever I don't want to be found."

She grinned back. "Better watch it, Bar. Secrets aren't secret anymore if anyone else knows them."

Johannes checked the charging indicator. It read seventy-five percent. Good enough, so he unplugged and coiled the cable in the car's trunk. "Back inside everyone. If things go well, we could be eating cold pizza with Max in well under an hour."

He merged back into the continual flow of traffic on the interstate. It was always busy, but this time of night, traffic at least moved along. Daria placed her hand in his lap, and he gripped it, lacing his fingers with hers. There were so many things he wanted to say to her, but Barney would feel the magic if they slipped into telepathic speech. And he might feel excluded.

Taking a breath, Johannes said, "I'm planning on setting our infirmary up in Max's office on the top floor. It's easy to protect because we can block off the elevator and the stairwell. Plus there's roof access and a hovercraft if you have to get out fast."

"Maybe. Being in the sky feels like flashing an 'I'm a sitting duck' sign. Where will you be?" Daria asked.

"One floor down in Audrey's office. That's the one with a million access points."

"If we're barricaded in, how will all those reinforcements be able to help us?" Barney asked.

"I told him about them back at the underground's headquarters," Daria cut in. "Figured he had a right to know before he decided on coming with me."

"There's no easy way inside. They'll have to fight their way through whatever shows up," Johannes muttered. "One shifter is worth at least a hundred humans, so it shouldn't be much of a contest."

"I'll keep my fingers crossed," Daria's tone was serious, "for all of us."

"Want me to tune into Max's broadcast?" Johannes asked.

"Yes," Daria and Barney both said.

Johannes fiddled with the car's onboard computer. Moments later, Max's voice filled the cabin, complete with a series of images on the screen that Johannes couldn't watch too closely and still drive.

"Damn, he's a good speaker," Barney mumbled from the backseat.

Johannes agreed. Listening to Max's rendition of the murder, torture, and subjugation of their kin, backed up with graphics and spreadsheets, filled him with helpless fury.

The city limits sign flashed by.

"Only another few minutes," Barney muttered. "Do either of you think this is going too well?"

"What do you mean?" Daria asked.

Johannes made eye contact with Barney in the rearview mirror and saw him shrug. "I don't know, exactly. But this is the smoothest damn trip I've had between the Bay Area and Sacramento in the last five years. Either everyone is glued to Max's broadcast, we got exceedingly lucky—"

"—or someone is herding us," Johannes finished for him. "Not much we can do about it, if that's the case. We need to play this one through. At least I do."

"Whatever you're thinking, it's a no," Daria cut in.

"I could leave you two at either of the big hospitals. They can always use extra personnel."

She clamped down on his hand. "No. If things go to hell, they'll have hacked into enough databases to know Barney and I are shifters."

Johannes took the next exit. Four more blocks to the state capitol. "I'm surprised medical dispatch would keep those kinds of records. It's our organization."

"They don't," Barney said. "But it hasn't been all that long since we were free people, and you don't have to hunt very long or very hard to figure out who has more than fifty percent shifter blood."

Johannes ground his teeth together. They'd made a good faith effort to obliterate what records they could, but there were still plenty they'd missed. With the sprawling complex of computer databases, scrubbing all of them hadn't been possible.

He turned the car into the garage and headed for the lowest level. Per his predetermined plans with Max. They'd take an internal stairwell. One of the back ones that lacked surveillance cameras. If things went according to plan, Loren, the head of Max's security detail, would be waiting to escort them upstairs.

Relieved to have the first phase in the bag—after all, it was when they'd been most vulnerable—Johannes drove down the spiral track leading into the bowels of the capitol building. He pulled into a parking spot at the very end of one of the aisles and hissed. "Stay inside. I'll get out first. Need to put one of my guns together."

"Do you want me to get out the one you gave me?" Daria asked in a strained voice.

"Probably a good idea."

"You never told me you were packing heat, Sata." Barney's voice followed Johannes out of the car.

Drawing magic to render himself mostly invisible—at least to those with purely human blood—Johannes popped the trunk and dragged his assault rifle from its case, snapping cartridges into it, once he'd attached the stock and sights.

"Johannes. Great that you're here." Loren came around a pillar. "You made good time." Another man shadowed him.

Of course Loren can see me. He has shifter blood.

Johannes hadn't actually forgotten that little fact, but it wasn't front and center, either. He wondered what else might've slipped his mind and winced. Scattering the magic shielding him, he asked, "Who's that?" and pointed at the man behind Loren. Worried about potential holes in his carefully crafted plan, he wasn't in the mood to make nice—with anyone.

"One of my men." Loren moved aside. "Step into the light, Bart, and let Johannes get a good look at you."

Once the man's hard bodied, dark good looks came into view, Johannes recognized him and lowered the assault rifle he'd had in firing position. "Thanks." He pulled his duffel out of the trunk and shut it with a *clank*. "Two medical personnel are inside the car."

Loren nodded. "I recognize Dr. Sata. She's been here before."

"Well then, you'll recognize her nurse too, once he climbs out of the back seat."

Walking around, he opened Daria's door. She got out, nodded at Loren and Bart, and ticked the seat forward, so Barney could exit the car with their medical supplies.

"Want me to carry anything?" Bart asked.

"We're good," Johannes replied.

"Well if you change your mind, just holler." Bart turned and led the way to a discreet door set into the garage's concrete walls.

"It's a lot of stairs," Loren murmured, motioning them to move between Bart and him.

"Go in front of me," Johannes told Barney. "Daria will go behind. That way one of you is sandwiched between Loren, Bart, and me."

He felt better when the door clicked shut behind them, and they started upward. Soon, very soon, they'd be in Max's suite of offices, which was pretty damned defensible—unless someone decided to blow up the building. Scenes from the World Trade Center disaster twenty years before played through his head, but he shut them down—fast.

Nothing could happen to Daria. Nothing. He'd waited millennia for a mate. That he'd finally found one was little shy of a miracle. He'd do whatever he had to if it meant keeping her safe.

If I really felt that way, I'd have hog-tied her and left her at the underground's headquarters in a broom closet.

"Good thing you didn't." Her mind voice vibrated with grim amusement.

"You picked a fine time to listen to my thoughts."

"I did, didn't I?"

Bart drew to a halt, and Johannes fanned his senses to full alert. They'd just passed the twelfth floor. Max's suite spanned the fourteenth and fifteenth, with roof access just outside his office.

"What?" Loren's voice was a low growl.

"Heard something," Bart muttered. "Quiet." He crept up the next few steps to the thirteenth floor landing and placed his ear against the metal door.

Johannes tuned into his cat's deadly sharp sense of hearing and asked, *"Do you hear anything unusual?"*

"Not sure. Wait," was followed by a pause so long, Johannes dropped to the step Daria stood on and stayed next to her, shielding her with his body.

"Men outside the next door, a few steps up," his cat said.

"How many?"

"Five, maybe six. With guns. I smell the metal."

Johannes made his way to Loren's side and placed his mouth next to the other man's ear. "It doesn't matter how I know this, but armed men are outside that door. Half a dozen."

"We can take them," Loren whispered back. "They won't be expecting us."

Johannes nodded. He focused his next words for Daria. *"Take Barney and the gun and make a run for the top floor. Do not go through any doors. Wait for me at the top."*

"Got it."

He waited until she and Barney were headed upward, moving silently as only shifters could, then motioned to Loren. They joined Bart on the landing, guns at the ready. Using hand signs, Johannes mimed counting to three.

Bart placed his hand on the reader and the locking mechanism snicked open. In one, fluid motion, he pulled the door open and darted to Johannes's side.

"Halt," Loren yelled before the door was fully open. "Building security. Show your passes."

Five men, dressed in black from head to toe, reached for weapons.

Johannes, Bart, and Loren opened fire. Seconds later, the five men lay in spreading pools of blood. Loren headed for one of them, but Johannes pulled him back. "They won't have ID. We need to get to Max and the rest of them. Where there are five, there are always more."

He pulled the self-locking door shut behind them and ran hard for Daria.

DARIA HUDDLED in front of the door with fifteen painted on it, gun clutched in her hand and pointed down the stairwell. She reassured herself nothing could happen to Johannes, but it didn't make her feel any better. Her stomach was sour, and the hot bite of acid etched into her throat.

The rattle of automatic weapon fire reverberated up the stairwell, driving her heart rate into hyper drive. She reached for Johannes through the mate bond, relieved beyond words to find him still in one piece. She wondered how his immortality actually worked. Did it make him immune to gunshot wounds, or simply give him the ability to survive any type of lethal injury.

"Shit!" Barney turned the word into a hissing mélange of sibilants.

She shook her head and mouthed, "Quiet." Part of her wanted to fly back down the stairs. Worse, her cat wanted out, convinced that if there was a battle, she was their logical form. Faster and far more lethal.

The door to the fifteenth floor flew open, and Max stood there, an assault rifle trained on them. "Jesus, damned good thing I looked before I fired. Johannes would've had my ass. Get in here. Both of you, and tell me what the fuck just happened."

"Keep the door open," Barney said. "Johannes will be along soon with Loren and Bart."

"Who were they shooting at?" Max asked. "Or was it someone else shooting at them?"

"I have no fucking idea," Daria replied and stepped out of the stairwell. She made a grab for equanimity, but it sidestepped her neatly. She tried to tell Max that Johannes was still alive, so if anyone was shooting, it was probably him, Loren, and Bart, but her teeth began to chatter from an overload of adrenaline.

Footsteps pounded from the way she'd just come, and she heard Max interrogating Loren.

Johannes grabbed her from behind and held her tight for a long moment. He smelled of cordite and fury. "That was an indulgence, but I needed to feel you against me. Let's get you set up somewhere I don't have to worry about you."

"W-where are you going to be?"

"I'm going to take Max with me and figure out how many infiltrated this building. We'll do it in our animal forms."

"We're going with him," her cat yowled.

A long claw poked through the end of one of Daria's fingers. She looked at her hand, horrified. Though she'd had several close calls, she'd never, never lost control before.

Johannes cradled her hand between his. "It'll be okay, Daria. You cannot come with us. Tell your cat why."

She understood why, so did her cat, but it didn't subside. Another claw pushed through.

"He's our mate," the cat insisted.

"Yes, I am." Johannes joined the mental conversation. *"I'm immortal. I can't die. You know that because my cat told you. Your job is to stay here and keep Daria safe for me, and yourself safe for my cat. We wouldn't want to live without you."*

"Not fair," her cat persisted, with an outraged yowl tacked onto the end of her words.

"No," he agreed, *"it's not."*

The pressure against her fingertips eased, and Daria inhaled raggedly as the claws receded.

Three men in security garb pushed into the office, a fourth slung between them. Loren hurried to their side. "What happened to Joey?"

"Took a slug down on floor two. Shit, boss, the place is crawling with commandos. Who the fuck are they? Where'd they come from?"

Blasted out of her funk by the only thing that could've gotten through, Daria crossed the room to the injured man. "Lay him down," she barked, followed by, "Barney, get over here."

"Yes, Sata." He dropped the bag and started fishing for a stethoscope and blood pressure cuff, handing them to her as he located them, along with latex gloves.

Daria snapped on the gloves and narrowed her focus to the man bleeding out in front of her. He had a gut wound with no exit hole, which meant the bullet was still lodged inside him. Judging from the black color of his blood, his liver was implicated.

Johannes knelt next to her. "I love you. Max and I are going hunting. We'll be back as soon as we can."

She glanced up from her patient. "Where are Kate and Devon and Audrey?"

"Holding down the fort at the computers one floor down, along with Josh and Abe. Ryan's with them. We'll leave a couple of the security squad to watch over you."

"Sata!" Barney's tone was sharp.

"Yeah, right here." She turned back to the man in front of her and went on autopilot. Barney handed her what she needed without her having to ask for it, which helped a lot. The next time she looked for Johannes, he was already gone.

The bullet was deep. She probed for it, missed, and hunted

again. This time, she hit pay dirt and extracted it gently from where it had been lodged in his liver. He was purely human, no shifter magic to leverage, so she shared some of her healing power, knowing if she didn't, he'd sink even deeper into shock and probably die.

"We're not supposed to do that." Barney said very softly.

She narrowed her eyes to slits and looked over at him. "You have any better ideas? I don't have IV equipment here."

He shook his head and wrapped shifter magic around them to shield their conversation from the guard. "Not that there's going to be any kind of medical board inquiry on this one, but if there was, I'd hate to see you get into trouble. You'd be outed for what we are, and that wouldn't be good."

Some of the tension in her muscles faded. "I care about you too, but I suspect the rules are about to change. If we win this war, all the things that they've forbidden over the past two years will go away, and we'll be back to business as usual."

"And if we don't win?"

"Then the world turns to shit around us and we go out in a massive, fucking flame war killing as many of those bastards as we can."

"I like your style, Sata." He loosed the power hiding their words.

"Good, because I've always liked yours. How's his BP?"

"Holding. He's still critical, but I believe he's stabilizing."

"Is he going to make it?" One of the guards who'd carried him in had been standing by the door, his hands clasped around his assault weapon so tightly his knuckles were white.

Daria looked up and saw a tall, well-built youngish man with a blond crew cut. He had the same, hard-eyed look as the rest of the security squad. She smiled and nodded. "I hope so. Let me inject him with some antibiotics and painkiller. He's unconscious now, but he should come around in the next little while."

"Thank God." The blond's face crumpled, but he got hold of himself before tears took over. "He's my little brother."

"Well, if we get through today, you should be able to take him home."

"Thank you. If you hadn't been here—" His face worked with emotion, and he swallowed hard.

"It's going to be okay." Daria returned her attention to the man on the floor. How were Johannes and Max doing? She hadn't heard any more gunfire, but she wouldn't have if it happened many floors down.

"You should take your own advice, Sata." Barney's voice was rough, pointed. "About things being okay."

She nodded and accepted a stack of sterile sponges from him to dress the man's open wound. Once she had them arranged, Barney handed her syringe after syringe of everything from opiates to antibiotics to dexamethasone, to mitigate shock.

When she glanced at her wrist computer, she realized she'd been tending to her patient for well over an hour. Where was Johannes? In fact, where was everyone?

As if in answer to her worried thoughts, someone knocked on the stairwell door right before it flew open. Kate and Devon raced into the room. A second guard, clearly stationed in the stairwell, pulled the door closed behind them.

"Time to go," Kate told Daria.

"Bullshit!" Daria retorted. "This man needs me."

"All hell is about to break loose out there," Devon said. "The cavalry's here, but so's our enemy. Johannes told me to get you and Barney out of here in the hovercraft. Audrey too. She should be in here any minute."

"Noted." Daria got to her feet and stared Devon down. "But I'm not leaving."

"Not that I'm more than a bit player here," Barney spoke up. "If Sata's staying, so am I."

"Told you." Kate shot a look Devon's way.

The door popped open again. Ryan sprinted through, with

Audrey right behind him. "Get them out of here," he barked, "so we can fight. My bondmate wants out now."

"Looks like no one's leaving," Devon snarled.

"Good," Audrey said, steel in her voice. "I didn't give Max any shit, but I have no intention of going anywhere." Her red-blonde hair fell across her face, and she swept it out of the way.

A grim, bloodthirsty grin cut across Ryan's stark features. "Great. Let's rumble."

"I can't leave my patient," Daria protested. "He's barely clinging to life, and he needs us, which means I can't spare Barney, either."

"Not a bad idea. Having both of you stay right here, that is," Kate said thoughtfully. "There will be more wounded."

"Fine," Devon said. "We have a plan, a field decision. Come on Kate. Let's kick some serious human butt."

"Hey!" Daria called after them. "Could one of you tell us what's happening?"

"No time," Ryan said. "If there's a break in the action..." He twisted to face Audrey. "I get it that you're not leaving the building while Max is fighting in it, but could you please stay with Daria and Barney where we have guards to watch over you?"

"Yeah. I'll stay. Either here or one floor down in my office." Audrey blew out a harsh breath. "I'm no warrior. Thanks for not forcing me out of here against my will."

"Welcome." Ryan motioned to Kate and Devon and they bolted back down the stairs, pulling the door closed behind them.

Daria stared after them before sinking back to where her patient lay on the floor. Not knowing was hard, yet she understood why no one wanted to take the time to fill them in.

"I've heard some of it over my communicator," the guard who'd thanked her for saving his brother's life said. "I'll tell you what I know."

"That'd be great," Barney answered for her.

"And I know things too," Audrey put in. "Between the two of us, I'm pretty sure we have a fairly complete picture. I can spare a few minutes to tell you what I know before I go back down to spell Josh and Abe."

Daria reached for Johannes through the mate bond. All she saw was blood. Rivers of it. His cat tore from one human jugular to the next, bathing in streams of crimson and higher than a kite on adrenaline. With difficulty, she wrenched her attention to the security guard and Audrey's tale, listening as it unfolded.

CHAPTER 11

An Hour Before
Johannes left Daria tending the wounded man and ran lightly one floor down.

Max was already in wolf form, his white Russian wolf coat resplendent. "Good job with the vid feed broadcast," Johannes told him.

Abe and Josh glanced up. Abe grinned. "Thanks, dude."

Max's wolf growled.

"Yeah, I'm going to shift. Give me a second. Where are Kate, Devon, and Ryan?"

"They went to check on reports of commando activity on the first floor," Audrey answered.

Max growled again. Louder this time.

Johannes understood. He shucked his gun and his clothes and shifted. He and Max hadn't hunted together in a long time, and it felt good to know he'd be running with his friend by his side. Even better to be heading into battle with him. He hated to leave Daria, but taking her straight into danger with him was unthinkable.

She was doing what she was clearly born to do, and so was he.

Max's wolf ran to the door and reared up, clawing the reader plate.

Audrey hurried to his side and placed her palm on the reader, then stood aside as Max sprang through the opening.

Johannes's cat was hot on his heels. *"We'll be methodical about this and sweep every floor."*

"Sounds good to me."

The remainder of the fourteenth floor was clear, so they used the public stairwell to move downward. *"Where's Boris, Carlos, and everyone else?"* Johannes asked.

"Five of the cadres are either in the garage or within five minutes of the building."

"And the other five?"

"On their way. Two ran into problems at airport security." The wolf whuffled softly. *"Guess someone didn't like all their weaponry."*

Johannes digested the information. Five thousand tough, armed men would be damn near impossible to hide. By now, the presence of even some of them had likely alerted the city's police, never mind Max's vid feed broadcast.

"It doesn't feel quite right," he said to Max, *"but unless someone has at least fifty percent blood, they're dead men."*

"We'll see. Depends who we run into. I know many, many of this building's occupants, and we're not killing my friends."

"Got it, but if something's going down, I won't be able to wait for you to ID if they're friend or foe." Johannes halted at the door leading to the thirteenth floor. *"Be alert. Here's where we killed those five."*

Max pushed ahead of him and vaulted through the door he'd opened with his mouth. Once inside the interior hall, he stopped, muzzle lifted, scenting the air.

Hackles raised the length of Johannes's back. Before he could say a word, Max took off at a dead run down a side hall.

A hail of bullets ripped from multiple assault rifles. Johannes ignored all of them and leapt at one of the men, tearing his throat out with a combination of teeth and claws. Between himself and

Max, they soon stood in a circle of death with a dozen men bleeding out from multiple lethal wounds.

Max's wolf leapt from side to side, grinning wickedly. *"This is incredible. I feel the bullets, but they're an annoyance, and then they go away."*

"We can do a victory dance later. I don't sense anyone else on this floor. Do you?"

Max trotted away from the carnage and raised his muzzle. Johannes joined him. It was hard to smell anything except blood, shit, and guts close to the dying men.

"One office has people in it," Max announced.

"At this hour, they're probably part of the crew we just killed. Let's get them." Johannes bolted down the hall, following a faint scent trail.

"Not necessarily. It's a media firm, and they keep odd hours. Let me take a sniff." Max passed him, halting before a frosted glass door. He turned toward Johannes. *"They're okay. I know them."*

Johannes didn't like it, but killing just to be safe didn't sit well, so he followed Max back to the stairwell. Partway down, the wolf halted, clearly listening to something.

"What?" Johannes nudged Max with his snout.

"Boris was checking in from the first floor. Six of our cadres are here, and the National Guard is pouring in to take us on, along with the city cop squad."

"Do you think we should clear the rest of the floors in the building before we go down to help our kin?" Johannes asked, still aiming for methodical.

"Probably," Max agreed. *"Two more shifters added to a few thousand won't matter a whole hell of a lot, and maybe we'll find something lethal up here, like a bomb."*

Johannes didn't know if Max's words were prophetic, but the rest of the floors were clear—until they hit the fourth. After mowing through fifteen men, they uncovered a nasty looking incendiary device linked to a timer.

Johannes shimmered back to human to gain access to his hands.

"Fuck!" Buck naked, he stared at the complex mechanism ticking away in front of him.

Max shifted too. "Tell me how I can help."

"I need tools. Even better, I need someone who knows something. Since you've got channels open to Boris, Carlos, and whoever else is here, ask if they have any bomb experts."

"How much time do we have?" Max asked, his voice terse.

Johannes bent and peered at the primitive timer. "I don't fucking know. Maybe not much. It's not digitized, so it's hard to tell."

While Max put out the call for help, Johannes rummaged through the empty office in search of a toolkit. Anything was better than what he had, which was exactly nothing. Finally, he located a set of screwdrivers and a hammer, wrenches, and pliers in a broom closet.

The door burst open about the time he was bending over the bomb, intent on seeing if it was as easy as just clipping a wire or two.

"Tatsky!" Max cried. "Good to see you, you old bastard."

"Save the greetings." The other man—tall, burly, gray-haired— knelt on the floor next to Johannes and trained his deep brown eyes on the ticking nightmare. He drew a leather-wrapped packet from an inner pocket and flicked the tie, spreading an array of tools that looked like dental picks between them.

Max kicked the door shut and joined them.

Tatsky jimmied one of his tools beneath a connector. "Hold this," he said. "Make sure the red wire doesn't touch the green one beneath it."

Johannes did as instructed, barely breathing while the Russian clipped wires and dismantled things, working fast and sure. He wanted to ask a million questions, but didn't want to break into the other man's obvious concentration. Sweat beaded on Tatsky's forehead, and he cursed in Russian when it sloughed into his eyes.

Time dripped by, but it wasn't more than five minutes before the Russian rocked back on his heels and swiped his forearm across his forehead. "Done. Are there any more of these bastards in the building?" he asked in heavily accented English."

Johannes realized the insidious ticking had stopped. "I'll be damned!" He hugged the Russian. "You did it. Thanks!"

"Other bombs?" Tatsky asked again. "We got this one by the skin of our teeth."

"We didn't find any between the roof and this room, but we didn't check the rest of this floor or the ones below it."

"None at street level." Tatsky got to his feet. "I did a sweep after we arrived."

"That leaves the rest of this floor and two and three, then," Max said.

Tatsky eyed them. "You two should shift. You can smell better in your animal forms. Besides," he chuckled, "we wouldn't want to give the female soldiers fighting with us heart attacks once they laid eyes on your dicks."

"Always the joker." Max slugged Tatsky's arm before the air around him turned liquid, and his wolf stepped out.

Tatsky wrapped an arm around his neck and they wrestled briefly. "Always the pretty one," the Russian teased Max. "That white pelt of yours got you more pussy than was good for you."

"You're just jealous." Max bared his teeth in mock play.

Johannes made a grab for his cat, and followed Max's wolf and Tatsky out the door.

The third floor was clean, but the second floor yielded a companion bomb buried beneath layers of files in a storage closet. They'd never have found it without Johannes's cat's keen sense of smell. Because it was the same design, Tatsky made short work of it.

"What do you think?" Max, still in wolf form, asked. *"We're about to join the fighting one floor down. Are we better off in animal or human form?"*

Tatsky paused. "Most of us have shifted, so I'd stay as you are. Only reason I'm human is Boris sent me to help with the bomb."

Johannes waited while Tatsky undressed and found his bear. The three of them swaggered down a winding staircase into the thick of things. Not much in the way of gunfire met his ears, and he wondered if the others had won the day while they'd been sweating over defusing bombs. Since he had a moment, he reached for Daria through the mate bond, relieved beyond words she was still where he'd left her.

Still safe.

Because he couldn't resist reaching out, he said, *"I love you."*

After a startled pause, she said. *"Love you too. Hurry back to me."*

"As fast as I can, darling."

Carlos ran to them. A sleek, black jaguar, he was beauty in motion. *"Do you have medical personnel on site?"*

"Yes. On the top floor," Johannes answered.

"Max, can you open the elevators so we can use them?" Carlos nudged him. *"We tried, and they're either locked or coded."*

"Yeah, I had security lock them. Grab your wounded and follow me."

A man with a gun rushed them from the right. Johannes leapt, driving him to the ground. His gun went off, but Johannes closed his teeth over the man's hand. He dropped the gun before Johannes shredded his throat.

Tatsky stood over him. *"He shot you point blank. Why aren't you dead?"*

Johannes shook blood off his snout and got all four feet under him. Time for damage control. *"Nah. He missed."*

"No. He did not miss." Tatsky bowed low, his shaggy bear's head sweeping the ground. *"I saw the spray of shells enter your body. You must be the one. In Russia, we've told tales of the first shifter forever. The one who cannot die."*

Before the bear totally blew his cover, Johannes hissed. *"Quiet. There's a story, but now's not the time or place."* Maybe by the time this was over, Tatsky would've forgotten.

Not very fucking likely.

A group of city police in full riot gear stormed through the glass doors.

"Come on." Johannes jerked his snout toward the new arrivals. *"Let's make them sorry they were ever born."*

~

DARIA STARTED when the elevator doors swooshed open. Max—a stark naked Max—gestured men and women carrying a variety of wounded through. Audrey was still in the infirmary, and she ran to him, hugging him to her.

"Watch it," Max said. "I have blood all over me."

"I don't care." Audrey clutched him harder before opening a closet and handing him a towel, slacks, and a sweater.

"Hey!" Barney got to his feet. "Look at all this work. They're singing our song, Sata."

"No kidding." She got up too, and together they did a hasty triage of who to put where."

After the fourth elevator of wounded, Daria asked Max, "How many more?"

"Not sure. I didn't do a count before I unlocked the elevator. I see the problem, though."

"Yeah, I'm going to need another room if this keeps up."

"I'll go back downstairs and try to get an estimate for you," Max said.

"Can I do anything?" Audrey asked.

He nodded. "Sure. Go by your office and make sure Josh and Abe are still on top of the vid feed. So far, all it's netted us are troops and cops. What I want are outraged masses turning out to support shifters. And news media. I'd love to have a whole circus of them memorializing the carnage downstairs."

"They'll come." Audrey's voice was laced with hope that arrowed straight into Daria's heart.

When she let herself think about them, the last two years had been hell. Living a false life. Always scared someone would find out and imprison her. Daria went back to triage and wound stabilization. At least it was something she had control over.

Max disappeared down the stairs. He was barefooted, but at least his body was covered. Daria supposed he'd left his shoes one floor down.

"Sata. Over here," Barney called.

She threaded her way to where he sat on the floor next to a very pale woman. A cursory examination didn't yield any wounds, so Daria dug deeper. "Crap!"

"What?" Barney bent closer.

"She's pregnant, or she was. Her body's absorbing the fetal material."

"Fascinating. I've only seen that a time or two. What can we do to help her?"

"Not much." Daria fisted a hand but stopped shy of slamming it into the floor. "I don't have the hormones that would halt the process—or the ones to hurry it along."

"It's a carryover from our animal sides, huh?"

"Yes. All female animals have ways of doing something similar if they're under attack." She placed her hands over the woman's uterus and fed shifter magic into her, linking to the woman's own innate power and strengthening it.

"There. Maybe that'll help."

"Aw, shit." Barney's head swung to the elevator door that had just opened again. "Many more and we'll need to see if there are any other medical personnel fighting downstairs. Maybe they could switch roles and help us."

"Depends. At least so far, no one's critical, except maybe this one." She patted the woman in front of her and infused more magic into her abdominal area.

Barney got up and hurried toward the elevator, no doubt to see to the new arrivals.

She stayed put. He'd call her if he needed her, and her current patient was fragile. Just because shifters could absorb their young didn't mean it was wise. Most had moved far enough from their animal companion's roots that things like this didn't bode well. She was certain the woman hadn't done it on purpose. The reabsorption was her body's spontaneous reaction to being under fire.

"Hold up there," Barney said.

Something about the tone of his voice drove Daria to her feet. She watched three more wounded being carried out of the elevator. Why had Barney told them to stop?

She sent her cat senses spinning outward, and her stomach clenched. These weren't shifters. None of them. "I'm the doctor here." Daria hustled forward, covering her fear of impending disaster with action. "Put those men down wherever you can find floor space, and then please leave my clinic. I'm short of space just now."

"Johannes!" she cried through their mate bond. *"Help me."*

"But—" Barney began, sounding agitated.

"It's all right. We'll make space for them." She shot a meaningful look his way, hoping to hell he'd read between the lines.

Anything to stall until Johannes showed up. The twenty-three shifters on her floor were mostly helpless, and she suspected the three men being carried weren't wounded at all. It was all a ruse to get into her clinic and engage in wholesale slaughter.

"I was going to suggest they take them to the hospital," Barney cut in smoothly. "It's only a few blocks down."

"Since when did hospitals begin treating shifters?" One of the men inquired.

"I frequently work there." Daria squared her shoulders. "I'm in the habit of saving lives, not inquiring who they belong to."

Her cat writhed within her. It knew what they faced, and it wanted battle, wanted to taste the hot copper of blood, wanted to roll in her enemies' deaths.

"Let me out."

"Not yet. Wait for Johannes."

"He's almost here."

The stairwell door slammed against its stops, and Johannes burst through in his cat form with a burly, dark brown bear by his side.

The three men dropped their burdens, who sprang to their feet, all of them reaching for laser guns hidden in the folds of their clothing.

Johannes and the bear launched themselves at the men. Barney shifted to the accompaniment of ripping cloth. He'd barely completed the transition before he'd driven his eagle's beak into one of the men's eyes. Shrieks, howls, and growls filled the room.

Daria's cat was done being subservient, and clothes shredded as she formed. Daria took stock of what they faced. Three men were still on their feet. So far, the others had fallen before firing a shot. They'd locked the elevator open, no doubt to stymie help from that quadrant, but it worked in Daria's favor because it meant more of their enemy couldn't use that route to access the top floor.

One of the men swung his weapon into firing position. Daria leapt on him, closing her jaws around his throat. The *phut-phut* of a laser pounded into her ribcage. It burned like mad, but she ignored it, intent on her kill. The man writhed beneath her, dying, but not fast enough for her taste.

When she finally let him go, the other two who'd remained were dead too. She let go of her prey, and a low, thin moan rippled from between her jaws.

Johannes bolted to her side, shimmering into his human body. "Shit! Daria! You're hurt." He turned her gently, and his stark intake of breath told her everything she needed to know.

Barney flashed from eagle back to human and knelt by her side. "Fucking lasers," he grunted. "These were illegally altered to do maximum damage."

"Can you save her?" Johannes's question was spiked with pain, frustration, and helplessness.

Barney's hands flew over her, questing, prodding. She lay quiet beneath his ministrations, but whenever he touched her right side, she wanted to screech her pain to the skies. Her breath bubbled and she tasted blood. She knew what that meant. Her lungs were hit. Once they finished filling with blood, that would be it. Thank God she was in her cat form.

"I love you," she told Johannes.

"I will not let you die." The words tore from him in a hot tide. "Hand me something sharp," he ordered Barney.

The other shifter obeyed, but questions mirrored in his eyes.

Johannes made a quick cut in one wrist and let his blood drip into her wounds. "Forgive me, Ceres." The words were low, muttered, but she heard them with her sensitive cat hearing. "I cannot let my mate die. I will not. If you want to punish me, so be it, but Daria cannot die. Not today. Not ever. I just found her, and I will not let her go."

"Thank all the gods we're in my body," her cat murmured.

"I'd be grateful too," Daria told her, *"because I love you, and I'd never want my death to cause you pain, but we're not going to die."*

"Bondmate. We're dying. Our lungs were hit. Twice." Her cat's voice was filled with sorrow. *"Somehow, I must find a way to go on without you, though I don't want to."*

"You won't die." Johannes joined their mental conversation. *"God help me, but I just made both of you immortal."*

"This is the same thing you did to save Max, isn't it?" Barney's voice held an awed edge.

Johannes nodded sharply once.

"Can you tell me what it is?" Barney's eternal fascination with all things medical shone through.

"I know what he did." The bear shifter was in his human body again. "This one." He bowed his head reverently and placed a hand on Johannes's shoulder. "He is the one our legends are made of. He is the first of us, and the goddess gifted him with immortality."

"Guess he let the cat right out of the bag," Daria murmured sleepily. Now that the struggle to draw breath had eased, she felt as if she could sleep for days.

"Don't you worry about a thing." Johannes moved his arm away from her side, and Barney wrapped gauze around it.

"Just going to let the blood flow ease up," he told her. "I think the slugs went through, but I want you stronger before I probe or hunt for exit wounds."

"Someone trained you well," Daria tried to joke, but couldn't quite pull it off.

"Not just someone. The best. Tell your cat to relax. I'll give you something for the pain."

The air brightened until Daria had to squinch her eyes shut.

"What is that?" her cat asked.

"I have a feeling we're about to find out," Daria replied.

CHAPTER 12

Johannes recognized the goddess presence. It had been millennia, but the feel of the ancient one was unmistakable. He rose and turned to face the pulsating luminescence, bowing his head. "Ceres. I apologize for breaking our covenant. The first time was accidental. This time, I used my blood to save my mate, with full knowledge of what I was doing. If you must punish someone, punish me—"

"Oh shut up. You always liked the sound of your own voice."

Johannes stood tall. If she was going to strike him with lightning or spirit him to wherever the gods had sequestered themselves, he was ready. At least Daria, his mate, his love, his heart, would live. Anything he had to endure was worth that gift.

Tatsky bowed low. "Goddess, you honor us with your presence. All of us wondered if you still lived."

"And where would I have disappeared to?" she inquired haughtily. "My kind are immortal."

"Of course, of course, my queen," the Russian murmured.

"This conversation is for my firstborn and myself only," Ceres announced.

Johannes felt power surge through the room, wrapping him in a vortex. Would the next thing be the vortex spiriting him…elsewhere?

"Given your actions, we must revisit our agreement and come to a meeting of the minds," Ceres said without preamble.

"Yes, goddess."

"I will forgive your trespass against our covenant, but only if it stops here."

Johannes thought about it. "I appreciate your leniency, truly I do."

"But, what?" she inserted before he was done talking.

"It's not a secret anymore. Max knows, though he'll keep his mouth shut. Tatsky is a different story. To him, I'm an urban legend come to life. I have a hard time believing he won't return to Russia and build shrines to me, the immortal shifter. Barney, the eagle shifter, knows too. At least enough to put two and two together. And then there are the twenty-odd patients lying on the floor, many of whom may have been listening when Tatsky voiced his suspicions."

"I will erase their memory of what they witnessed today."

"That fixes one problem," Johannes agreed. "What about Max and my mate?"

"So long as they never breathe a word, I will be satisfied. You were quiet for millennia. No reason they can't be too."

The conversation was going remarkably well, so Johannes took a chance. "Goddess, would you hear me out? I promise I'll be brief." If he'd been able to see anything beyond pulsating light, he was certain Ceres would be rolling her eyes.

"Brief being the operative term. Say what you will."

"When you first created us, your infinite wisdom was wise to ensure we wouldn't live forever. Things have changed in the last two thousand years. A lot of things. There are fewer of us. Some species, like ravens and foxes, have died out. Many of us gave up on finding our mated one, because the mate bond has become exceedingly rare, so we've mated with humans, diluting our blood.

We have very few children in any case, whether mated to shifters or to humans—"

"But if I lift my ban, and all of you tap into immortality, those problems will disappear within a few hundred years."

"Maybe not." He spoke thoughtfully. "I'm not sure quite where you've been, but Earth is going to hell. The water and air barely support life, anymore. Most of the fish have died off because of red tides and the ocean growing too warm to sustain them." He hurried on. "What I'm saying, is we need all the edge we can get."

"I'll consider your request, firstborn."

"I don't believe all shifters will want the gift, and of course it would only be available to those with more than fifty percent blood, those who can shift."

"How would it impact those like Max's mate, who were created with serum?"

She may not have been here, but she has been paying attention.

"Of course I've been *paying attention*." She sounded irritated.

Johannes took care to blank out his mind, so a stray thought wouldn't annoy her further.

"Wasn't one of your plans to offer that stuff to everyone with a dram of shifter blood?" the goddess went on.

"It was, but if Max's plan to blow the lid off our persecution works, we won't need to."

Ceres sighed, and wind whistled through the vortex. "Modern life has made things terribly complicated. I will not be making any far-reaching decisions today. For now, I will wipe the Russian bear's memory, and that of the eagle shifter and those scattered about on the floor. You will alert Max and your mate to keep their mouths shut."

"Understood. Thank you."

The shining light shattered around him, and he was back in the infirmary in the midst of slaughter, the hot scent of blood thick in the air.

Barney looked shell-shocked, but he was still bending over Daria's cat, making certain she was mending.

Tatsky shook himself. "Odd," was followed by a spate of Russian.

Johannes didn't inquire too closely, fearing he might undo whatever magic Ceres had spun.

"How's Daria?" he asked Barney.

"She's healing. If she'd taken those laser slugs in human form, she'd have been dead, but her cat's stronger than crap. It pulled her through." He shut his eyes for a moment. "Thank God. She's the most talented healer I've ever met. It would've been a crime to lose her to senseless violence."

"Do you think she's well enough for her human form?"

Barney shook his head. "Not quite yet."

"Want me to help you get these bodies out of here?" Tatsky asked.

"Yeah, We can huck them onto the roof. Make it easy for the meat wagon to send a hovercraft to grab 'em."

"Why bother?" Irony thickened Tatsky's accent further. "I say we dump the sorry sacks of slime off the edge."

Johannes agreed in concept, but falling bodies wouldn't help their cause. He said as much before he shouldered one of the dead, realizing he was still naked. Good thing. Blood was hell to get out of clothes. By the time he returned from his third trip, Barney was sluicing the floor with water.

Tatsky muttered the whole time about how soft Americans were, how unused to primal violence. Not wanting to get into an argument with the Russian, Johannes didn't say much.

Tatsky prodded Johannes in the ribs. "I am returning to the battle. Nothing more for me to do here." The air took on a liquid, glistening aura, and his bear formed. With a final jostle from his snout, he waited while Johannes unlocked the elevator and set it to open on the first floor.

"Daria's still stable," Barney said, anticipating Johannes's next question.

"Thanks for letting me know. I'm leaving, but I'll be close enough to yell for, and I won't be gone long. Just going to grab my clothes one floor down and check how the vid feed's coming along. It's been damned quiet from Josh, Abe, and Audrey."

Barney gave him a thumbs-up sign, and he melted through the doorway, intent on figuring out what came next. If the battle that had been raging out of control when he ran to help Daria was still going strong, they'd need another strategy—or more troops.

He burst through the door into what had once been Audrey's office. It probably still would be—if they won. "How goes it?" He headed for where someone—probably Audrey—had folded his clothing neatly over the back of a chair and proceeded to climb into underwear, his trousers, and his shirt and sweater. He balanced on one leg to pull on socks.

"You're mighty quiet," he observed.

"We're still transmitting," Audrey said.

"Barely," Abe muttered. "Bastards have tried to cut us off bunches of times."

"Good thing we got that schematic of how the vid rolls in and out of here," Josh said. "It's given us alternatives when we've needed them."

Audrey's wrist computer beeped. She glanced at it, and her mouth formed an *oh* of surprise.

"What?" One shoe on, the other in his hand, Johannes bolted to her side.

"It's the press. What should I do?"

"Answer it," Johannes said, levering his other shoe on. "This might be one of the breaks Max was hoping for."

"Shit! Given the mess downstairs, something has to break loose, or we'll never get out of here," she said before tapping her display. "Governor's office." Her voice was crisp. If she was nervous, she hid it well.

"Put it on speaker," Johannes mouthed.

Audrey nodded and made the adjustment.

"Is this Ms. Weston?" a male voice asked.

"Yes, it is. Who am I speaking to?"

"Whew!" Relieved male laughter. "This is Kevin McGrady from United Press Corps. We've spoken before, and I was hoping I had your correct contact info."

"I remember you, Kevin. How can I help you today?"

"Is the governor available for a press conference? Some of the reports rolling out of his office are—" he paused "—somewhat hard to believe."

Johannes bent toward her. "This is Johannes Takes. I'm head of the governor's personal security team. Before you ask, I can reassure you our governor is safe. At least he was an hour ago."

"The allegations." Kevin stammered something unintelligible, and then found his voice again. "They can't possibly be true."

"They are," Johannes said. "Via a combination of sleight of hand and an egregious misuse of power, shifters have been targeted for death for the last two years. It's gotten much worse over the last six months. Law enforcement is killing shifters before booking them in jails and prisons—to avoid the cost of feeding and housing them."

Kevin sputtered. "I'd love to get an exclusive with the governor. Is he available for a press conference? My team can be there in under ten minutes."

"How?" Audrey broke in. "Our lobby's turned into a war zone."

"The press has immunity."

"That won't help if a stray bullet finds you," she said tartly.

"This story is big enough, I'll chance it." Kevin's voice rang with male bravado.

The elevator opened, and Max walked in. His longish hair had escaped its habitual queue, and he looked trashed. "Who's on the communicator?" he asked, striding toward Audrey.

"Is that you, sir?" Kevin croaked.

"If by *you*, you mean California's governor, yes, it's me. Who's there?"

"McGrady from UPC," Audrey answered.

Max's face broke into a broad smile. "Great. Glad you took the time, Kevin. I suppose you want validation for my broadcast."

"We do, sir. And I'd love a face-to-face."

"Tell you what." Max's transition from weary warrior to consummate politician happened so fast, Johannes blinked in surprise.

"Anything, sir. I'd love to get an exclusive—"

"Not going to happen. This is too important to my people."

"Your people?" Kevin gasped. "So the reason you're doing this is because you're a shifter? Can I quote you on that? Or was it off the record?"

"I'm done hiding," Max said flatly. "Done standing by while my blood kin suffer. The deal is this. Take it or leave it. You can land on the helipad on the roof. Bring representatives from at least two other press consortiums, and I'll give you your news conference. In the meantime, I can send you supporting documentation to prove what's been in the vid feed since last night."

"Awesome. Great. I'm on it."

"Where do you want me to send the material?" Max chuckled softly. "We want to make certain everyone believes what you release."

Kevin rattled off an electronic address.

"Got it," Audrey said.

"Kevin," Max said. "One last thing. What my assistant will be sending you are classified documents. Here's the code you'll need to open them."

Kevin read it back, then said, "Thank you, sir. Appreciate the opportunity. Be there in a flash."

"I'll post a man on the helipad to let you in."

Audrey disconnected. Getting to her feet, she dragged Max into a hug. "What's happening downstairs?"

"At least the flood of cops has slowed to a trickle. Ditto for the National Guard. Boris is squaring up for round two, but I'm hoping it never happens. That call from Kevin is a good thing. A very good thing. It could make all the difference."

"What do our losses look like?" Johannes asked.

Max grimaced. "More than I would've liked. The loss of even one more shifter life costs us all. We have fourteen dead. A few more wounded are heading for the infirmary." He glanced at Johannes. "What happened? For a while, the elevator wouldn't work, almost as if someone had locked it open."

"They did," Johannes said through clenched teeth. "Come upstairs with me, and I'll fill you in. We were attacked. Daria called me through the mate bond, and…" He grabbed a gun on the way out of Audrey's office. So did Max.

"I want to hear that story too, eventually," Audrey called after them.

By the time they walked into the infirmary, Max had punched the wall several times. "Bastards," he gritted through clenched teeth. "To take advantage of our wounded hits a new low, even for them."

Johannes glanced at where Daria lay. She'd morphed back to human form, which he took as a good sign. He wanted to go to her in the worst way, but she seemed to be sleeping, and he wasn't done talking with Max.

Barney put a finger over his lips, and came close. "She's resting," he whispered. "How many more patients can I expect?"

"Three or four," Max replied, keeping his voice low. "None of them are in very bad shape."

"Great. No need to rouse Daria. Not that she could do much more than bark orders right now, but still, I'd like to let her rest."

Johannes motioned for Max to follow him and headed for the hallway leading to the helipad. Once they were out of earshot, he hit the high points from Ceres's visit. By the time he was done, Max's blue eyes shone with wonder.

"Son of a bitch. So she's real after all. Not that I didn't believe, but…"

"I know. I'll stay out here and greet the press. Walking them through our infirmary will be great for some photo ops. Then I'll bring them down to Audrey's office."

"I'll be ready for them." Max grinned. "This was a gamble, but damn if it's not working out. I feel it in my bones. We'll be out from under their fucking yoke—and damned soon if I'm any judge."

Johannes watched him walk back down the hall. It was hard to hang onto his natural tendency toward pessimism in the face of Max's passion. He hadn't realized it, but Max was a natural-born politician. He loved people, listening to them, working to improve their lives. By a twist of fate, he'd ended up exactly where he belonged.

Johannes stifled laughter. Max was a glad hander, and he was a spy, loving the shadows and digging up dirt.

"Good thing we each have our gifts," he muttered.

He unlocked the door to the helipad and settled in to wait, gun at the ready. Who knew which hovercraft would drop out of the skies? It surprised him the attack hadn't moved from ground to roof much earlier in the game.

In the first few moments he had since Ceres's visit, he thought about the goddess. What would she decide about his request that all shifters were at least offered the choice of immortality? Had he brought it up to ensure an end to his enforced loneliness?

No. Because I'll have Max and Daria no matter what.

He grinned wryly. Apparently, he'd had an altruistic moment. They cropped up every now and then.

The sound of a motor drew his eyes skyward. One of the larger hovercraft was heading right for the roof. Johannes stared at it. No press credentials on the doors. He backed into the shadows to wait. They must've seen him, but that was his own damned fault. He shouldn't have been out in the open.

Had the call from Kevin been a sham? Was it just a way to move the war to a second front?

Johannes made a split second decision and tapped a few keys on his wrist communicator, requesting backup. He might not need it, but if he did and hadn't called, things could get ugly really fast. If bad guys were in that craft, he'd be hard-pressed to hold the door by himself.

Silver skids kissed the rooftop and a door popped open.

Johannes sucked in a tense breath, his gun ready, safety off. The weapon he'd scooped up was an old-fashioned .45 semiautomatic. Lots of stopping power, but he didn't have a spare clip.

Gotta make every bullet count. If it comes to that.

"Get out of the bird nice and slow," Johannes called. "Hands up and away from your bodies where I can see them."

"Jesus!" A woman with long, red hair peeked from around the door. She teetered on ridiculously high heels and was dressed in a charcoal business suit and bright red blouse. "Don't shoot me by accident."

"Everyone else out." Johannes wasn't taking any chances. Women were commonly employed as decoys.

After a breathless scramble, six men and two women stood in front of the hovercraft, hands held in front of them. Johannes sent his cat senses scattering wide, and relief filled him. No other life in the craft.

Behind him, the door slapped against the building's concrete wall, and four male shifters raced out, flanking Johannes.

"Any trouble, boss?" one of them asked.

Johannes glanced his way. "Not yet."

"We have cameras and recording equipment in the hovercraft," the redhead said. "Can we please get our gear before we meet the governor?"

Johannes motioned the shifters forward. "Clear out their stuff for them. Make certain none of it's a bomb masquerading as something benign."

"You got it, boss." The shifters surged into the hovercraft, handing things out to waiting hands.

"Careful with that camera," one of the press corps muttered. "It cost five thousand credits, and I can't replace it. They don't make that kind anymore."

"Craft's clean," one of the shifters shouted to Johannes. "Nothing else in there. No bombs."

"Shit!" Another man muttered. "You guys really play hardball."

"You would too if people were trying to kill you," Johannes countered. "Does everyone have everything they need?"

After a series of nods, he motioned the group inside. If even one of them was a commando masquerading as a journalist, they'd be in a world of hurt.

CHAPTER 13

*D*aria had progressed to sitting up, propped against a wall, when the flock of journalists stormed her infirmary, snapping photos and asking questions. Barney had found her a clean pair of scrubs, but her feet were still bare.

"Are you the doctor here?" a redheaded female journalist asked Barney.

"No. Dr. Sata is the physician. She's on the floor over there. She was wounded by commandos who came up the elevator pretending to need medical care."

The redhead's eyes widened. "Really. They were that underhanded?"

"I don't know why you sound so surprised." Daria let sarcasm fly free. "None of this is new. It's just more visible than it's been. The fuckers almost killed me."

Johannes hurried to her side. "You don't have to talk with them," he murmured. "Save your strength."

She shook him off and struggled to her feet. It still hurt to breathe, but not that much. She stalked to the journalist. "We bleed just like you do. We can be killed just like you. I'm a doctor, sworn to protect life. Shifters are living creatures. We deserve respect, not condemnation. What's happened to us is criminal, but what's worse is none of you did a thing to stem the tide."

"W-we didn't know," the journalist stammered.

A middle-aged man with thinning dark hair walked to her side. "We also didn't look very hard," he said. Something like shame crossed his face. "I was grateful I didn't have much shifter blood, but I'm rethinking that."

"Yeah, what we did to shifters is a whole lot like what the Nazis did to the Jews," another journalist chimed in.

"That's a hot angle," another man piped up. "I'll use it when I write this up. Genocide right under our noses. Just like all those towns next to places like Dachau and Auschwitz, where the inhabitants claimed they knew nothing."

A wave of dizziness swept over Daria and she leaned into Johannes, who'd followed her across the room. Part of her was appalled the journalist was hunting for pithy angles, but a deeper, more practical side was into whatever worked to bring their plight into plain view.

"Be sure you get pictures." She spread her arms wide.

A high, thin cry burst from the other female journalist, and she fell to her knees next to one of Daria's patients, a young wolf shifter who'd taken a bullet through his upper leg, shattering the femur.

"Paddy. Oh Jesus Christ, it is you." She laid a shaking hand on his shoulder, but he didn't stir. "He's still breathing, but he's so still. Is he—?" Her blue gaze locked on Daria's face.

"He's sedated," Daria said. "He'll make it, but he lost a lot of blood before he got to me, and I don't have transfusion equipment here."

"I can see he's transported to a hospital."

"Why do you care?" Johannes's voice was so rough, it startled Daria, and she got a snapshot into the depth of his hatred for the humans who'd reduced them to this.

"He's my stepson. I raised him." Strong emotion, maybe guilt, turned her cheeks crimson. "I knew he was more than half shifter, and when the purge started, I just hoped he'd be okay."

Daria read between the lines. "You kicked him out, didn't you?" She stopped shy of adding *to save your own sorry hide.*

The woman's eyes swam with sudden tears. "God help me, I did. Shit! This is my fault. My responsibility."

"Pull yourself together, Pam." The other woman dragged her upright. "We have a job to do here, and if we do it right, maybe you can at least partially redeem your sins."

"Maybe so." When Pam straightened her shoulders, she looked ten years older.

Max chugged through the stairway door. He'd changed into a dark suit, white shirt, and red tie. His hair had been brushed back from his face into a queue, and he radiated a take-charge attitude.

"I thought we were having a press conference." His sharp, blue eyes swept the room. "I'm ready for you."

"And we're ready for you, sir. I'm Kevin." The man with thinning, dark hair stepped forward, his hand extended.

Max grasped it. "Yes, I recognize you. And many of the rest of you too. Did any of you have a chance to review the data I sent to Kevin?"

Amid a low murmur of voices, the journalists followed Max down the stairs.

The four hatchet-faced shifters who'd herded the journalists in from the helipad crowded after them, their guns still drawn. No one was taking any chances.

Daria dropped into a chair, still feeling weak as a kitten. "How are things going in front of the building?" she asked Johannes. The flow of wounded had stopped, but that didn't necessarily mean they were out of the woods.

"Yeah." Barney came close. "I'd like to know too."

"I'm not sure," Johannes answered. "It's been quite a while since I left the worst of things." He draped an arm around Daria. "I'd go look, but I'll be damned if I'm leaving my mate's side again—ever."

"Sounds good to me." She ginned up a smile. "Hey, Barney. How about if you call dispatch. Maybe they can get someone up here to spell me. I'm not worth much, and I likely won't be for a day or two."

"One step ahead of you, Sata. I already did. A relief doc should be here any minute."

"Great." She smiled wanly. "Maybe they can give us an update from downstairs." Her words registered in her fuzzy brain. "Aw shit. They have to go through that mess. Hope they're able to get to us."

"The penalties for mowing down medical personnel are severe," Barney reminded her. "Otherwise none of us would ever go anywhere."

She wanted to say more, but weariness tugged at her. Even her cat was quiescent, healing. The sound of the elevator snapped her out of a semi-doze.

A tall, thin woman with very short black hair strode through the door, carrying a medical bag. She wore teal scrubs, twin to Daria's, and thick-soled black shoes.

"Zoe!" Daria tried to get up, but the other woman motioned her back down.

"Stay put, Daria. Let me get a good look at you." The woman's dark eyes were pinched with worry as she ran her experienced hands over Daria. Tugging up her scrubs, she examined her wounds, sniffing with her wolf senses and probing with her human fingers.

Finally she spared a glance at Barney. "You did good work here. Probably saved her life."

"Thanks." An embarrassed flush turned Barney's face almost the same shade as his hair.

"Fill me in on everyone else." Zoe turned her attention to Barney. "Before you start, though, are you able to stay to help me, or should I order up another nurse?"

"I can stay," Barney said. "It'd be an honor, Dr. Greeley. I've heard a lot of good things about you over the years."

She snorted. "Flattery doesn't work on me, young man. Walk me through who we have here."

Daria turned to Johannes. "I'd like to go home. Is that even a possibility? Not my house in San Francisco. It's too far away, but yours."

"I honestly don't know. How about if we listen in on Max's pitch to the journalists, and then I'll see if we can't hitch a ride in their hovercraft."

"Sure. I'd like to hear what Max has to say too." She let him help her out of her chair. "Maybe by then, we'll be able to get to our car in the garage."

"Maybe so," he agreed, but he might've been humoring her because he didn't sound hopeful. His next words clinched it. "Even if we made it to the parking garage, the streets have all been cordoned off. Driving is off the table—at least for now."

"Before we leave." Daria faced Zoe Greely. "How'd it look when you came up from the first floor?"

"Like the war in Kosovo." She grimaced. "But things were definitely either winding down or in one of those lulls where both sides are sick of killing each other, so they take a break. I was able to make it up the stairs and into the building—and across the lobby— with no one bothering me."

"Well, we'll hope they're winding down," Johannes said. "Daria. Can you manage one flight of stairs?"

She nodded. "Sure. Probably good for me to move around a little."

"Not too much," Zoe cautioned. "What you need more than anything these next twenty-four hours are sleep and liquids."

"Yes, doctor." Daria attempted a salute and ended up giggling at how badly it turned out. "Shouldn't have given me so much painkiller," she told Barney.

"Enjoy it," he advised. "It won't last that much longer."

Johannes steered her toward the stairs. When they got there, he swept an arm beneath her knees and lifted her, cradling her body against him.

"Put me down."

"I don't think so." He carried her carefully down the twenty steps to the next floor.

She heard the hum of voices and the whirr of vid feed recording equipment long before they got to the bottom. Max, in true oratorical form, was bathed in light from vid feed cameras. His words, every movement, and his regal bearing were captured and broadcast to the far reaches of the state, the United States, and all corners of the world.

"I'm really proud of him," Daria spoke low near Johannes's ear.

"*I am too,*" he switched to telepathy through their mate bond.

"*You didn't think this would work.*"

No. I didn't, but I supported Max because I didn't see where we had a choice. Not when the enemy started smoking us out and killing us." His mind voice held a fierce edge.

Daria wound her arms more tightly around his neck. "*I love you. I'm lucky to have you.*"

"*We're lucky to have each other. Hush. I want to hear the last of Max's speech. He seems to be building up to something, and if I know statesmen, he'll cut it off after he makes a few more points.*"

She considered asking to be put down again, but it felt so good in Johannes's arms, she snuggled closer. They stood off to one side toward the back where they could listen, but be unobtrusive and hopefully beat a retreat while the press peppered Max with questions after he was done talking.

"...don't want to cover the same ground twice, but here's a quick recap," Max was saying. "I won't be taking questions afterward. Everything you need to know was in the material I sent to Kevin and what I've said this past half hour."

"Are you really a Russian wolf in your other form?" the redheaded journalist took a few steps closer, naked hunger stamped on her face.

"He is." Audrey stepped between them. "He's also my mate."

"Oh," the journalist muttered. "Figures he'd be taken." She didn't retreat to her earlier position, though, and continued staring at Max as if she wanted to divest him of his clothes right there in front of everyone.

"And I said no questions." Max sounded stern. "My mate answered that one, but neither of us will be answering further ones.

"Here's that recap. After a gang war in Florida two years ago, someone decided shifters were responsible for everything going wrong in this country. A second bloody gang conflagration in New York fed ammunition to the rumor mill. An extraordinarily conservative contingent decided the only good shifter was a dead shifter, so they began working behind the scenes, leveraging power where they could."

He stopped to take a breath. "Given the lack of decent air and clean water, everyone was looking for someone to blame. Shifters became the fall guy. Never mind, we're all environmentalists at heart. Most of us were alive in better times, and we remember the luxury of stepping outside and filling our lungs with pure, clean air.

"It wasn't a quantum leap from there to where we found ourselves today—"

"Sir!" Abe materialized from deeper within the room, ducking beneath the line of cameras trained on Max.

"Can it wait?" Max asked. "I'm almost done here.

"You'll want to see this." Abe sounded extremely excited, given his usually laconic nature. "The public must be listening to the vid feed from all these news people, or maybe your earlier feed finally reached critical mass. People are storming the capitol. The streets are thick with them, and more are arriving by the moment."

Johannes didn't wait to hear more, he moved to the bank of monitors at the far side of the room.

"You have to put me down now," Daria said. "I want to see."

He set her gently on her feet and stood next to her with a protective arm around her body.

She bent to look at the displays. "Oh my God!" Her throat thickened with tears that spilled down her face. The streets were mobbed with people, many of them carrying placards, all demanding freedom and equality for shifters.

Audrey was by their side, looking too. "Fantastic!" She fist pumped the air. "Phenomenal! It couldn't possibly be any better than this." And then she was crying too.

Max joined them, took a quick peek, and then returned to his spot in the limelight. "A heartfelt thanks to every single one of you who are here with me today at the capitol. You heard my plea. You believed me, and you're voting with your presence. Blessings on every single one of you. Today we've made history. You should be proud to be a part of it."

Max made a curt, unmistakable hand signal, and the journalists cut their machinery.

"It's Friday, but I'll be in my office all of next week," he told the press corps. "Feel free to make an appointment if you want to talk further with me."

He headed for the elevator.

"Where are you going, sir?" Kevin asked.

Max turned a blinding smile on him. "Those are my people out there, son. I'm going out to greet them and thank them personally."

"Not without me, you're not." Audrey hurried to his side.

"Yeah, well, you're not going without protection, either," one of the four shifters from the helipad said, and they piled into the waiting elevator with Max and Audrey.

Johannes made his way to Kevin. "Any chance of you folks dropping Dr. Sata and me off at my house with your hovercraft? We'll never get out of here by road. Or at least not anytime soon."

"Sure." Kevin was grinning broadly. "Jesus, but Max is one gutsy bastard. To go out there when there could still be a sniper with a gun trained on him… It's beyond brave."

"We need to include that in our broadcast, before we wind it up," the redhead said. "And then we'll be out of here."

"Dr. Sata and I will wait for you on the roof," Johannes told her just before he lifted Daria again and carried her back upstairs.

"How'd it go?" Barney looked up from a patient he was bending over with Dr. Greely on the other side.

"Better than good," Daria said. "Max is well on his way to becoming an urban legend, and humans demanding our freedom are storming the state capitol."

"It's about fucking time," Zoe snapped. "This whole thing had gotten way out of hand."

"Thank you," Daria said.

Zoe glanced at her. "For what?"

"Being here for my patients."

"Pfft. It's nothing, Sata. You'd have done the same for me." She narrowed her eyes to slits. "If I'm not mistaken, that man with you in his arms is your mate."

Daria tried not to smile, but couldn't pull it off.

Zoe got to her feet, covered the distance to them in a few quick strides, and wrapped her arms around them both. "Congratulations. Best of everything—to both of you. It makes my heart glad to see mated pairs. We don't have nearly enough of them these days." She stepped back and made shooing motions with both hands. "Now get out of here. I don't expect to see you anywhere for at least a couple weeks. You never take vacations, and once you're better, you and that dreamy cat shifter should honeymoon somewhere your cats can romp and play."

"Sounds like doctor's orders to me." Johannes quirked a brow her way.

"It does make it hard to say no." Daria leaned into him, breathing in the clean, pure scent unique to him.

He walked through the door on the far side of the room and on out to the helipad where the hovercraft waited.

When she looked beyond the rooftop, every single street was choked with humanity streaming toward the capitol. "Look." She pointed. "Oh my God. Just look at all that."

"I see." He set her down, wrapped his arms firmly around her, and kissed her, but gently, as if he was afraid she might break. When he lifted his lips from hers, he said, "This is the first time in a long while I've felt hope for the future of our kind. Damn, it feels good. I didn't realize how far I'd sunk into a sense of hopelessness. I kept going, but—"

Daria placed a hand over his mouth. "I know exactly what you mean. My heart is glad today. Glad for you and our mate bond, but also glad for our people."

The journalists trooped out onto the helipad, and everyone got inside the hovercraft, carrying their recording equipment. Daria claimed a window and watched as the craft rose into the skies. For at least five miles around the capitol, cars and people on foot flowed forward. They all wanted to see Max. To hear him, to touch him.

Almost as if he'd read her thoughts, Kevin turned to her. "Max. He's a magic man. Wouldn't surprise me if he ended up President someday."

Next to her, Johannes snorted back a laugh.

"What?"

"Max would like that," he said into her mind. *"Let's not suggest it to him, huh? Last place I want to move is Washington, D.C."*

CHAPTER 14

Week Later

Johannes dished up his latest creation, whistling merrily. He was just parceling it onto a plate, preparatory to carrying it upstairs to Daria when she walked into the kitchen.

"Sweetheart." He put his utensils down and walked to her, sweeping her into a hug. "Are you sure you should be up and about?"

Daria cradled his face between her hands. "I'm well. Healed. Ready to go back to work."

He winked. "It's all that sex therapy."

Laughter bubbled from her, the sweetest sound he'd ever heard.

"That and all the hours we've spent as cats roaming the grounds. Regardless. I can't just lie around anymore."

He gazed at her and kissed her forehead and eyelids before letting her go. "That other doctor said for you to take a couple weeks off—"

"Zoe did say that," Daria agreed, "but I don't need that much time."

"Maybe not for your work, but how about for us? We could go somewhere. I haven't had any R&R, either. For a long time."

"Doesn't Max need you here?"

Johannes thought about it. The last week had spawned a series of miracles, starting with a general apology to shifters from no less than the U.S. President. Followed by offers of funds for any shifter who applied for them, to make up for the loss of jobs and property since the purge began.

"Probably not," he replied thoughtfully. "There are still a few commando groups convinced the new laws reinstating full and complete freedom and rights for shifters are a mistake, but those types have always existed in the shadows."

"True enough," she agreed and snapped up her plate from the ledge. "Since you made this wonderful entrée, let's figure out what happens next over dinner."

He nodded, readied a plate for himself, and joined her at the kitchen table with an unopened bottle of merlot and a corkscrew. After a cursory glance, he put everything down and went to retrieve wine glasses.

She'd already begun eating. "Sorry," she murmured once she'd chewed and swallowed another mouthful. "Healing has been hungry business. Seems I'm always hungry these days."

"Mating is hungry business too." Just thinking about her made his cock hard.

She reached over and patted his erection. "Can it wait until after we eat?"

"It better. The other option is twitching up your skirt and turning you over the table."

Daria smiled, and the world melted into sexual heat around him.

"We could do that too. You choose."

He pushed his cock to a better position and sat. "You need food. I'm supposed to be nurturing your convalescence, not sabotaging it." He opened the wine and poured some for both of them. "Sex aside, Max and Audrey should be home soon."

"Did we leave enough food for them?"

"They already ate. You asked if Max still needs me. The worst of things are over. We'll be doing damage control for months, but you and I could slip away for a week."

"Where would we go?" She raised her glass his way. "To us and to freedom for our kind."

"Great toast." He clinked his glass against hers. "I'll drink to that. I've thought about where we could go. If we had more time, I'd like to show you my home in northern Greece, but I think it's a little early in the amnesty game to push the envelope with international travel. Plus, I haven't been there for a long time. Place might not still be in one piece."

"Probably wise." She drew her brows together into the line that meant she was thinking about what he'd said.

Johannes couldn't stop looking at his mate. She was such a beautiful creature. Perfect in every way.

"Love the adulation, but you need to eat before the wonderful meal you made gets cold."

He took a few bites. The stroganoff mixture had come out well, and he silently thanked Max for having the foresight to set up farms and grow rooms to make sure they'd have access to real food.

"Is there a place you'd like to go?" he asked Daria. "If this will be like a honeymoon for us, we should choose it together."

"How about the northern California coast? I've always loved the area between Mendocino and Fort Bragg."

"Brilliant! It's close enough we can come back if anyone needs us, but far enough away, maybe they'll think twice."

"The coastal forests are still thick, so our cats could run." Daria drained her wineglass, and he refilled it.

"We could leave tonight." He made short work of the rest of the food on his plate, anxious to spirit her away now that they'd decided.

"We could. Do you want to take a hovercraft or a car?"

He thought about it, and poured himself more wine. "Maybe a hovercraft. That way we'll have more time on the coast and less fighting traffic."

"Perfect." She sent a coquettish glance his way and reached beneath the table to lay a hand on his leg. "Do you know exactly when Max and Audrey will show up?"

"No. Want me to find out?" At her nod, he tapped a few keys. "They haven't left the capitol yet. Max held an impromptu late press conference."

"That was the right answer." Daria stood and opened the embroidered silk kimono she'd wrapped around herself. Staying tantalizingly out of reach, she pirouetted, displaying her body from every angle, but not taking the kimono all the way off.

"Come here, wench." He pushed up from the table and dragged his top over his head. Next, he toed off his house shoes and pushed his sweatpants out of the way. He wasn't wearing underwear. His cock stood out from his body, thick with need and more than ready.

"I want a turn," his cat spoke up.

"You had one an hour ago."

"I don't care. Since when is there a moratorium on how much sex I get?"

Daria laughed. "My cat's pitching a fit too, but this time we're going to stay human. I want to feel your tongue all over my body and your fingers. And a few other things too." She ran her tongue over her lips. "Found some of your toys." She pulled a vibrating cock ring from one of her pockets before she let the robe slip from her shoulders.

"Want to experiment with it?" He made a grab for the silicone ring, but she held it just out of reach along with something else he couldn't quite see.

"I get to put it on you."

He closed the distance between them and crushed her to him, stringing kisses down her face and neck before closing his mouth over one of her nipples. She splayed her hands across his back, kneading the muscles of his back and ass. She spread his butt cheeks and tickled his anus with a finger that rapidly shifted to a small dildo.

He gasped with pleasure as she inserted the vibrating cylinder inside him. Tearing his mouth from her breasts, he managed to ask. "What else did you find?"

"I'd rather surprise you."

The stimulation against his prostate was almost more than he could stand. "You have something in mind. Do it, or I swear I'll take you where you stand."

She wriggled out of his grasp, tugged a chair over and sat, spreading her legs to give him a view of her pussy. Keeping the dildo inside him, she took his erection in her mouth. Between the miniature dick exciting him from inside and her other hand and mouth on his shaft, semen shot from him, but the climax didn't make a dent in his arousal. He held her head while she licked up his jism, pleased when she slipped the cock ring on his still throbbing penis.

"That works best if it's against your clit." He reached around and pulled the toy from his anus. Without waiting for her to say anything, he scooped her into his arms and carried her into the sitting room on the far side of the kitchen where he laid her on a sheepskin rug. Her hair spilled around her like a dark, glistening halo, and her lips were parted, her breathing fast.

He wanted to start with her toes, like he'd done before, but he was too excited. She writhed beneath his touch, and he slithered down, so his mouth was over her core. He stopped shy of touching her, breathing heat microns from her sensitive nub. Her hips bucked, and she grasped his head between her hands, jamming her sex against his mouth.

Johannes could take a hint. It was hard to tease her for very long because he wanted her even more intensely than she wanted him. He closed his mouth over her clit, sucking hard and sank fingers inside her. A few firm sucks and a thorough tongue lashing, and her vault convulsed around his fingers.

He rode her climax through before moving up her body and sinking his cock into her. She locked her knees around his waist and her arms around his shoulders, nails digging into his back. The vibrations from the cock ring added spice to his already voracious need for the woman in his arms. Knowing what the toy would do to her, he shimmied close, making certain the silvery nub contacted her clit.

She gasped. "Oh my God. That's intense. I've never used toys."

Johannes kept the pressure tight against her until he felt the spasms of her next climax around him. Then he withdrew and teased the sensitive circle of nerves around her opening. She rocked against him, clearly wanting the clitoral stimulator back in place. No reason they couldn't both have what they needed. He balanced on his arms and drove into her, glorying in the scorching heat of her around him. The cock ring held blood in his penis and intensified everything.

Daria shrieked her delight and clawed at him. His cat was close to the surface too, offering ribald suggestions. Johannes danced along the edge of his next climax, doing everything he could to stave it off, to draw it out. When she tightened around him for a third time, he gave up and let himself fall over the edge and into a paroxysm of delight. Pleasure coursed through him, and he finally closed his eyes, but still saw Daria spread beneath him, her golden skin dusky with lust, her dark eyes liquid with wanting him.

He let himself down atop her, heart thudding against his chest. The cock ring still vibrated, and he knew they could go several more rounds.

"We're bringing the toys with us." She laughed. "I found some other stuff too. Maybe we could bring it all."

Johannes nuzzled her neck, snorting laughter. "Glad there are some things they don't teach you in med school."

"And I suppose I'm glad I'm mated to a total pervert."

"Let's get up and get moving. We could be at the coast in time to watch the sunrise." He kissed her and got to his feet, stripping the ring off himself and hitting the off switch.

"I'll pack us a few things." She accepted his hand to help her up and grabbed her robe, securing it around herself.

"And I'll clean up down here. Don't want to leave a mess."

"I love you. Perverts have always been my thing." She collected the cock ring and dildo and stepped to the sink, rinsing them with soap and water.

"Now you tell me." He swatted her rump. "See you back down here with our stuff."

"You got it. I'm excited we're going somewhere. Thanks for pushing me into doing something beyond my obsession with medicine."

"Anytime, darling. Anytime."

DARIA MADE her way dreamily up the stairs. Sex with Johannes just got better and better. It was hard to imagine how she'd ever go back to a job that kept them apart for hours—let alone days—at a time. She'd go mad if she didn't have access to his body.

He and I will find a balance. I don't want to quit work, but maybe I could tell them I want to cap it at twelve-hour shifts...

She smiled to herself. Being mated was a whole new ball game, and they'd just take things one day at a time. The important thing was knowing Johannes would be by her side now and forever more. She'd been jealous when she found the sex toys—until she found his vid feeds and realized he'd spent far more time masturbating than indulging in sex with women.

After a quick shower, she threw things for both of them into a suitcase and made her way back downstairs. When she walked into the kitchen, Johannes was deep in conversation with Max and Audrey.

The other woman ran to her and hugged her. "I'm so glad you've decided to get away for a few days. God knows, you deserve it."

"I'd love to take Audrey on a honeymoon," Max boomed. "Maybe after the two of you get back, we'll manage something."

Audrey rolled her eyes. "Yeah, separating you from the capitol will be one neat trick. Maybe in a year. Not in a week."

Max gazed fondly at her. "So long as you don't love me any less."

"How could I? You're my mate, and I love you exactly the way you are. Remember, I worked for you for a long time, worshipping you from afar and all that." She walked into Max's outstretched arms.

"What'd Human Resources say about you continuing to work for Max? Wasn't that meeting sometime earlier today?" Daria asked. Since Audrey let it slip that she was Max's mate at the press conference, it had become widespread knowledge.

Audrey made a face. "They said I could stay until the end of Max's current term, but that if he gets reelected, he'll need to find a new administrative assistant."

"By then, you'll be pregnant and have other priorities." Max grinned.

"You don't know that," Audrey protested.

His smile broadened. "Maybe I have inside information."

"Probably a good note for us to leave on." Johannes draped an arm around Daria and led her out of the kitchen. They made their way through the large, silent house and out into a night drenched in moonlight.

"Oooh, I'd forgotten the moon would be full tonight." Daria stopped to gaze at it.

"It'll be even more beautiful over the water. Let's hurry. We'll take Max's hovercraft. It's bigger and faster, and he offered it."

"Nice of him." Daria trotted after Johannes to the landing pad.

"Yeah. Self-serving too. If he needs me back here, he wanted to make sure I could return in a hurry. I don't suppose any of us will totally trust the amnesty deal until more time has passed. After you." He stood aside while she got into the hovercraft. "I swore I'd never ride in another one of these, but now that the unrest has settled down, it seems like it won't turn into a tension-riddled nightmare."

"I sure as hell hope not." Concern for him filled her. "We don't have to go tonight if it makes you uncomfortable."

"Nah. It's all good." He made his way to his seat. "Just my conservative nature coming to the fore. All those years as a spy gave me a slanted view of human nature."

"Well, I have forever to improve your attitude. In case you've forgotten."

"I haven't."

She snorted. "I'm afraid my outlook isn't much better. There's something about putting bodies back together—after someone shot them or knifed them—that doesn't exactly yield a staunch belief in mankind's inherent goodness."

"Yet one more place we're well matched. We can shore up each other's pessimism." He settled behind the controls, and the craft lifted smoothly into the night sky. "Since you mentioned the immortality gig, I figure I'll hear something from Ceres about my pitch to include all of us, but it could be years."

"Or maybe not ever."

"Why not?" He turned and his face, illuminated in moonlight, was so profanely beautiful, she wanted to drop to her knees and worship him.

"Maybe she's like me and has a hard time saying no."

"Not the goddess I met."

"It's been what? Two thousand years plus since you saw her the first time?" At his nod, Daria went on. "Time is different for her. It might be another few thousand years before she shows up again."

The smile on his face dimmed. "Do you think the planet will last that long?"

"I have no idea." Daria thought about it. "Mankind is pretty enterprising. Something will survive, but I bet it looks a whole lot different than what's here now."

He reached over and clasped her hand. "I'm sorry I brought it up.

This time is for us to be happy, not to worry about a future we don't have much control over."

She laced her fingers with his, content to be by his side. "That's the coast range, isn't it?" She pointed below them.

"Yes. This bird is fast. Twice as much airspeed as the smaller models. We'll be there very soon."

"Any idea where we'll stay?"

Johannes shook his head. "None, but even if we bed down with blankets in the back of the hovercraft, I'll be a happy man."

"Not a bad idea. At least it's private. More so than a motel would be."

"You got it. We'll camp tonight and see where tomorrow takes us. Look at the moon on the water."

She drank in the golden orb's reflection, and an idea bloomed. "Could we take a moonlight walk on the beach?"

"I don't see why not." He fiddled with the controls, and she watched as the ground came up to kiss their skids.

Daria unlaced her shoes. She wanted to feel damp sand between her toes.

"I want out too," her cat demanded.

"Can we?" she asked Johannes.

"Maybe. If no one else is there. I know there aren't any more prohibitions against shifting, but I don't want trouble, either." He took his shoes off and followed her out of the hovercraft into a damp, mild night.

She threaded her arm around his waist and they walked into the surf. The salt tang of the air tickled her nostrils, and she breathed deep. The ocean might be polluted, but it still smelled like it always had. Surf pounded against her legs, wetting her pants to the knees.

"It's beautiful here. Feels like we're the only ones in the world."

Johannes stopped walking and held her close. Cupping her head in his hand, he kissed her long and deep. When he lifted his mouth from hers, he said, "Want to shift?"

Daria nodded. To share the deserted, moonlit beach with their animals would make the moment even more perfect. She walked up the shore to a large rock and undressed, leaving a smaller rock over her clothes to make sure they wouldn't blow away if a breeze came up.

Her cat was close and the transition easy. The salt smell intensified tenfold. So did scents of small rodents hiding in driftwood littering the beach. Next to her, Johannes shifted too. His cat nudged her playfully, and they took off running for all they were worth, kicking up sand with their paws.

"Happy," her cat purred. *"So happy."*

"Me too," Daria answered her. *"This has been a long time coming."*

After so many transits of the beach, she lost count, Johannes shimmered back into his human skin. She did too, and they fell into each other's arms laughing and panting.

"I love you to distraction," he murmured into her ear.

"Love you too. Those blankets are sounding good."

He kneaded the globes of her ass. "That sounded surprisingly like a proposition, Dr. Sata."

"Smart man." She ducked from under his embrace and ran to where they'd left their clothes. When he got there, she handed his to him. "It was a proposition—the smutty kind—and I don't like to be kept waiting."

"Guess I'm flat out of choices." He made a face at her. "You have all my toys." He took a measured breath. "Except my very favorite one."

"Really?" She quirked both brows. "I was thorough. Don't think I missed anything."

"Darling." He stepped close and ran his fingertips down the side of her face. "You're the best toy of all."

Happiness surged, and she fell into step with him as they headed for the hovercraft. Knowing she'd be in his arms with his hardness buried deep in her body thrilled her beyond words.

Maybe it was the mate bond. Maybe it was Johannes. Maybe it was everything rolled up together.

"It doesn't matter what it is," he said, having been inside her head. "We have each other, and that's all that matters."

With her cat purring for all she was worth, Daria followed Johannes into the hovercraft. "Hey!" She made a grab for his ass.

"Yes?"

"If we hurry, maybe we can still watch the sun come up."

He spun to face her and reached to pull the hovercraft's door shut behind them. "We can have it all, darling. Nothing is beyond us. Not now. Not ever."

Before she could agree, he covered her mouth with his and kissed her.

Six Months Later

Johannes sat on a rocky outcropping looking over the rugged countryside in northern Greece. He and Daria had finally left California for a two week vacation. Max and Audrey had joined them this last week, but all too soon, it would be time to return.

Daria leaned into him and tightened the arm she had twined around his waist. "It's lovely here," she murmured. "Just lovely."

"Like a fairyland," Audrey agreed from where she and Max perched on a neighboring rock pile. "Say." She eyed Daria. "If you could pull yourself away from your mate for a few, I'd love to explore that bazaar in the village."

"How do you know I wouldn't be interested?" Max inquired archly.

"Because you hate to shop," Audrey retorted. "How about it, Daria?"

"Sure. I'm game. Maybe while we're there, we could find something interesting to bring back to the villa for supper."

Johannes's ears perked up. "Fish, if you can find it," he suggested. "Fresh greens. And a nice white wine."

"But you have hundreds of casks in your wine cellar," Daria protested.

"Indeed. Much of it went bad in the century I wasn't here." He shrugged. "I need to clear it out, but this is our time, and I didn't want to waste a moment on cleaning. That wine's been rotten for years. Tossing those casks out for the recycler can wait."

Audrey got to her feet. "Come on." Her eyes glittered mischievously. "We'll have a blast."

Daria kissed Johannes's cheek. "Back soon," she murmured. "It shouldn't take long to buy so much, we won't be able to carry any more."

"Buy whatever you want, darling." Johannes stood and held out a hand to help her up. "This isn't a time to scrimp."

"Oooh," Audrey squealed. "Permission. Let's hit it, Daria."

The women slipped their bare feet into sandals and trotted down a well-worn dirt track chatting and giggling.

Johannes's heart swelled with happiness, and he turned to Max. "It's wonderful they get along so well."

Max nodded. "Everything since I've been mated has been wonderful." He rolled his eyes. "Sheesh, that sounded hokier than hell, but I hope the wonder of it all never wears off."

"I suspect it won't." He settled closer to Max. "Have you decided about whether you'll run again?"

Max frowned. "I do have to either fish or cut bait—and damned soon."

"Want to hash out the pros and cons?" Johannes quirked a brow.

"You're not exactly an uninterested party."

"No. I'm not. You caught me dead to rights. I'm hoping you decide to sink into obscurity with your mate and have a few children."

Max rested his chin on an upraised hand. "I never planned to get swept up in politics. Didn't even think I'd like it all that much…"

"But it grew on you."

"Oh hell yes, it did. I haven't been this attached to anything I've done—ever."

Johannes narrowed his eyes to slits. "You have public opinion on your side. They all see you as some kind of latter day Joan of Arc. If you wanted to take a shot at the presidency, I'm fairly certain you'd win."

Max chuckled. "I could save the taxpayers hundreds of thousands of dollars by not bothering with the Secret Service, huh?"

"There is that. Except you're sworn to secrecy about immortality." Johannes took a measured breath. "On the other side of things, I'm selfish enough to want your talent and expertise for us, not humans."

"How so? We don't really need the underground anymore. In truth, I was getting ready to disband it."

"I wasn't talking about the underground."

"What then?"

"Our council of twelve could use shoring up. We rarely communicate unless there's a flat out crisis—"

A blast of power ripped Johannes's next words from his mouth.

"What the fuck?" Max bolted upright.

Johannes felt him gather power, felt Max's wolf just beneath the surface. For some reason, his cat hadn't said a word. Understanding flattened him and he stumbled to his feet. "It's the goddess," he told Max. "Daria didn't think she'd show up for hundreds of years —if ever."

Bright light pulsed around them. "Your mate doesn't know me very well," Ceres sniped.

"How could she?" Johannes countered, fiercely protective of Daria.

"Stand down. I wasn't criticizing her. You and I have unfinished business."

"I can leave," Max offered, sounding rattled.

"Not necessary, since you've become immortal through the meddling of my firstborn."

Johannes waited. Ceres would tell them what was on her mind when she was ready to, not a moment sooner.

Johannes's cat purred a greeting. Ceres purred back, then greeted Max's wolf as well. A fragrance reminiscent of summer wildflowers filled the air, and Johannes inhaled its healing scent, reminding himself the goddess's first love was animals. It was why she'd created shifters in the first place.

"I have given much thought to your request," Ceres said at length. "I conferred with others like me, and we focused our energies on Earth." She paused, perhaps for emphasis. "What we found shocked and saddened us. It may well be too late, but I am here to present you with an offer."

"Love to hear what it is," Max said in his best statesman's voice.

The brightness shifted until Max was illuminated. "This proposition is not up for discussion or negotiation. I can almost see wheels turning in your mind."

"Understood," Max murmured.

Johannes longed to encourage Ceres to just spit whatever it was out, for God's sake, but he kept his mouth shut.

"Better." The light moved again until it encompassed them both. "The gods are in agreement. We will offer immortality to any shifter with more than fifty percent blood—including those who've received that infernal serum—with the following caveats."

Johannes leaned forward, anxious to hear her terms. Next to him, Max's sharp intake of breath said the same. Of course, he'd want his mate to be immortal since he was.

"Good that neither of you are haranguing me with questions," Ceres said smugly.

"You're welcome." Johannes smiled. "You went to a great deal of trouble to come to us. You won't leave without telling us everything we need to know."

"That sounded suspiciously like something Max might've said."

Max stifled a snort.

"Regardless," the goddess went on. "The first caveat is no more serum. Forget you know how to make it. Destroy whatever stocks you have."

"Agreed," Max and Johannes said almost in unison.

"Next," Ceres said. "You must shore up your leadership. By this time a year from now, I expect to see shifters in key positions all around the globe, taking up the banner to salvage what we can of this planet. No more trusting humans to not totally muck things up. I created you to be the best of human and animal combined. At the time, I never dreamed how important it would become to leverage your gifts, but I understand it now."

"It would be a pleasure," Max said. "Johannes was just saying something rather similar before you showed up, er materialized, er…"

"Never mind," Ceres said dryly. "I understand."

"We'd be honored to take on that burden," Johannes said. "I've been worried about what would be left of Earth to support Daria's and my children."

Tinkling laughter cascaded around him. "That will happen sooner than you expect," Ceres murmured.

Joy broke over him, shattering his composure. "Is Daria pregnant?"

"Just since this morning, but indeed she is."

Johannes let out a whoop. "Sorry, that wasn't very dignified."

"Congratulations!" Max started to shake his hand, but ended up hugging him instead. "Amazing news!"

"The two of you can crow later." Ceres's tone edged into sternness, not unlike a crusty schoolteacher.

"Yes. Of course." Johannes untangled himself from Max and faced the pulsating light. "So far, no serum and shifters are to infiltrate themselves into key positions all over the globe."

"Exactly." Ceres sounded pleased.

"May I ask a question?" Max stepped closer to the brightness spilling toward them.

"Yes, but I may choose not to answer it."

"Fair enough. What if humans don't allow us to get that close to their various inner circles?"

"I have faith in you. Figure it out."

The light wavered, began to dim. "Wait!" Johannes extended an arm.

"Why? I've said what I needed to."

"But I need details," he sputtered. "How will other shifters avail themselves of immortality, for starters?"

"I will take care of that." Laughter chimed again. "Did you believe I'd allow the two of you to parcel out such an enormous gift?"

Embarrassment rushed through Johannes. "Of course not. I had no idea how it would work, but—"

"You're going to wait, aren't you?" Max broke in, focusing his words at the light.

"Huh? I don't understand," Johannes said. "Wait on what?"

"There's a reason you've done so well in politics," Ceres responded, clearly addressing Max. "Of course, I'll wait to make certain you destroy the serum and do the remainder of my bidding as well."

Johannes thought about her words. "If we've made a good faith effort by this time next year—"

The light blazed so brightly, he had to shut his eyes.

"No *good faith effort*," the goddess shrieked. "Either you will have complied—or not. If you truly care about the fate of your race, I suggest you find a way to make my requirements happen."

The light exploded, leaving a sharp afterimage dancing before his eyes.

"Holy crap!" Max made a noise that might've been a snarl. "I'll never fault myself for being highhanded ever again."

Johannes shook his head, still working to clear his vision. Once he wasn't seeing double, he muttered, "She didn't ask for anything unreasonable."

"No," Max agreed. "Frankly, I was surprised when she left. I assumed there'd be more to the deal."

"Don't underestimate what she requested." Johannes sent a speculative glance skittering Max's way.

"I'm not." He hesitated before adding, "I know what you're thinking."

"Do you now?"

Max's expression turned serious. "How's this? Close to accurate? We were just talking about what I'd do next, and I'm suddenly damned glad I served the stint I did in the governor's office. It's given me the skills I'll need to pull off the goddess's demands."

"Your term has another year," Johannes pointed out.

"Yes, but now I have a solid reason to quit. I didn't tell you, but I likely wouldn't have run for a second term, anyway. Not having Audrey next to me all day, every day, was quite the deal breaker, and HR only gave her a bye for the duration of the current term."

Johannes faced his old friend. "Are you going to quit once we return home?"

Max's face creased into a warm smile. "Do I have a choice? I'd love it if shifters could be immortal. What a goal to work toward."

Johannes's wrist computer vibrated. He glanced at it, and saw Daria's ID. "Hang on," he told Max and turned his attention to his mate, tuning in both audio and visual channels.

"Hello, love." She smiled brightly.

"Hello back. Bought out the store yet?"

"We're working on it," Audrey called from the sidelines.

"I called because I just heard from Barney," Daria said.

Johannes's stomach tightened. Would they have to cut their time away short? "Did something happen?"

Daria laughed. "Oh no. Nothing like that. Didn't mean to give you a scare. Turns out one of those eagle shifters from New Zealand —you know the ones Kate mentioned at headquarters—isn't related to him. The female eagle is as excited as he is. Nothing's been decided yet, and no one knows if there's a mate bond, but I'm happy for him and wanted to share the joy."

"Great news, Daria!"

"Yes," Max seconded. "Be sure to give him my best too."

"Will do," Daria said, sounding terribly pleased. "See you both soon."

"Love you."

"Love you too." She disconnected.

"Want to walk back to the villa?" Max asked.

"Sure. We have a lot of planning ahead of us."

"That we do." Max nodded.

Johannes gathered the blankets they'd been sitting on, folding them. Max took one, and they headed for the villa half a mile away.

"I was thinking," Max began.

"Always dangerous."

Max elbowed him. "Hear me out. This thing is too big for the two of us. What we'll need to do is get the other ten elected leaders on board. Ceres didn't say we couldn't tell anyone, and we'd almost have to if we're going to pull this off…"

Johannes listened as Max outlined the first phases of a plan that would likely undergo many, many alterations over the next few months.

"There are no coincidences," he said.

"What?" Max stopped midsentence. "You interrupted me."

"I know. When you decided you had to be California's governor, I thought you were flat, fucking nuts. What I see now is it was part of a larger plan that had to play itself out. You said it yourself, earlier. That it was a damned good thing you'd picked up a political skillset. All I'm doing is agreeing."

"Will you and Daria be part of whatever unfolds?" Max stopped at the gates leading into Johannes's villa.

"Of course, so long as she agrees. As long as you brought her up, please don't tell her about her pregnancy."

"Whyever not? I figured we'd celebrate tonight."

"Because I want her to figure it out and come running to me with the news. She might even know before we have to leave

Greece. Her cat will probably tell her. We agreed to try for a child a couple months back, so it won't come as a total surprise."

"We will tell the women about Ceres's visit, though."

"Of course we will. We want them onboard with whatever this next year brings."

"It's going to be an enormous amount of work." Max rubbed his hands together.

Johannes burst out laughing. "And you can hardly wait."

"You know me too well."

Johannes clapped him on the back. "Indeed I do. Now let's pour ourselves a nice glass of wine and toast the day when all of us will be offered the option to live forever."

"Best offer I've had for a long time." Max mock bowed. "After you, my friend."

Johannes tapped his wrist computer, and the gates of his estate swung open. Hope for the future of his kind burned bright within him. He had no idea if Ceres could hear, but he sent her a heartfelt thank you anyway.

You've reached the end of the Underground Heat Series. If you liked these books, you might enjoy some of my other paranormal romances featuring shifters. Dragon shifters play a key role in the Dragon Lore books. A sample follows from *Highland Secrets*, the first book in that series.

ABOUT THE AUTHOR

Ann Gimpel is a USA Today bestselling author. A lifelong aficionado of the unusual, she began writing speculative fiction a few years ago. Since then her short fiction has appeared in a number of webzines and anthologies. Her longer books run the gamut from urban fantasy to paranormal romance. Once upon a time, she nurtured clients, now she nurtures dark, gritty fantasy stories that push hard against reality. When she's not writing, she's in the backcountry getting down and dirty with her camera. She's published over 50 books to date, with several more planned for 2018 and beyond. A husband, grown children, grandchildren and wolf hybrids round out her family.

Keep up with her at www.anngimpel.com or http://anngimpel.blogspot.com

If you enjoyed what you read, get in line for special offers and pre-release special reads. Sign up for Ann's newsletter on her website or her blog.

BOOK DESCRIPTION: HIGHLAND SECRETS, A DRAGON LORE PREQUEL

Furious and weary, Angus Shea wants out, but no matter how he feels, he can't stop the magic powering his visions. The Celts kidnapped him when he wasn't much more than a boy and forced him to do their bidding. He's sick of them and their endless assignments, but they wiped his memories, and he has no idea where he came from.

Dragon shifters are disappearing from the Scottish Highlands, and the Celtic Council sends Angus to investigate. He meets up with Arianrhod, legendary virgin huntress from Celtic myth, in Fire Mountain, the dragons' home world.

Arianrhod prefers to work alone, mostly because she harbors a dirty little secret and guards her privacy for the best of reasons. She's not exactly a virgin, and she'd be laughed out of the Pantheon if the truth surfaced. Despite the complications of leading a double life, she's never found a lover who tempted her to walk away from her fellow Celtic gods.

Attraction ignites, hot and so urgent Arianrhod's carefully balanced life teeters on the brink of discovery. Angus is everything she's ever wanted, but he's far too close to her Celtic kin to keep her secret safe. Angus wants her too, but she's a Celt. He's hated them forever, and she's part of everything he's lain awake nights plotting to escape from.

Can they risk everything?

Will they?

If they do, can they live with the consequences?

Books in the Dragon Lore Series:
Highland Secrets, Prequel
To Love a Highland Dragon, Book One
Dragon Maid, Book Two
Dragon's Dare, Book Three

*A*ngus Shea stroked beneath icy waters off the northern tip of Ireland, blending his energy with a pod of Selkies. The sea creatures cut through choppy waves in front, behind, and above him. He'd rather dive and play in the deeps with them—and if it were any other day, he would have—but he needed to keep an eye on the skies, so he edged toward the surface, pushing his head free.

Celene, a coal black Selkie he'd done more than swim with, moved close enough her lush pelt stroked his skin. He draped an arm around her, and she nuzzled his neck with her snout.

"Where have you been?" She spoke deep into his mind. Accommodating vocal chords were part of her human form, not her seal, and he'd never learned the Selkies' lyrical language.

"I spent a little time at my home in Scotland, but mostly I've ranged far from the Irish Sea."

"That doesn't tell me anything." She nipped playfully at his shoulder with her squared-off teeth.

"Prying ears are everywhere." He leaned into her warmth, enjoying a respite from the cold water.

"We could go where no one would hear."

He was tempted, so tempted he toyed with saying yes and

taking a break from watching for the dragon he expected. Dragons interpreted time in their own way, and the damned thing might not show up today or tomorrow or even this week. If it showed at all.

How much could he tell the Selkie?

An answer crowded on the heels of his question.

Nothing.

Angus shuttered his mind, so the creature swimming by his side couldn't read it. Much as he yearned to talk with someone, anyone, about the impossibilities the gods tasked him with, prudence won out. Not that this assignment was worse than any of the others, but he'd finally figured out they'd never end.

I could say no. Tell them I'm done.

He cut off the bitter laugh that wanted out. Whoever had the balls to refuse the Celts risked swift and certain punishment. He could hear Gwydion, master enchanter, or Ceridwen, goddess of the world, laughing their heads off—before they cut out his tongue or killed him on the spot.

"You don't have to say a word." Celene went on, almost as if she'd peeked into his thoughts before he took care to protect them. Selkie laughter buffeted him, spraying him with a warm, rich melody mixed with salty water. *"I'm curious, but I miss your body."*

He missed hers too. She'd been his only break from solitude for more years than he wanted to admit. He cast another glance skyward. Though he tried to be subtle, he heard a smug murmur near his ear and knew he hadn't fooled the Selkie.

"You wait for an Ancient One." The tenor of her mind speech shifted as she shielded it from anyone who might be close. Without stopping for him to corroborate, she forged ahead. *"We can take up the banner and watch for you. My kin will let us know."*

Angus picked his way carefully, as if he walked through a field of unexploded ordnance. "I appreciate the thought, but no one can know of my comings or goings, lass."

"We know more than you think." Celene batted him with a flipper.

"In truth, very little escapes us, but here isn't the place to share what I heard about your latest mission."

Concern rippled through him. If the Selkies knew, who else might? Hell, he didn't know much beyond his assigned meeting place with the dragon, and they'd be heading into danger.

What else was new? Danger was so second nature, his adrenaline pumps barely flinched at anything these days.

"Come with me." Either Celene was oblivious to the turmoil rumbling through him, or she ignored it. She swam from beneath his arm and herded him toward shore. *"There's a secluded glade deep in marsh grass. No one will find us, and my kin will keep watch for the dragon. I already asked."*

The Selkies would do their best—and maybe today it would be enough—but they were no match for evil that had sunk its roots deep into the fabric of the Old Country and the rest of this world. It was why the gods stooped to using him—half-mortal, half-divine, or whatever the hell he was—to do their dirty work. Arawn, god of the dead, revenge, and terror, caught him skulking in the time-travel tunnels when he wasn't much more than a boy and trapped him, cutting off any possibility of return. To make certain Angus remained, the god altered his memories, so he had no idea where he came from.

Now almost twenty-five years later, Arawn and the others still came up with enough for him to do that a life to call his own was out of the question. The carrot they dangled was the truth about his birth, but they never came close to divulging it. The stick was his fear of what they'd do, if he told them he was done.

Over time, he'd stopped asking about his origins. He cared, but it wasn't worth the energy to run up against their stony faces and cunningly crafted half-truths that revealed exactly nothing. Despite his reservations about a quick dalliance with Celene—and maybe missing his rendezvous with the dragon—he was sick of his self-imposed isolation.

She chivied him into shallow water. Once she was certain he'd follow, she drew ahead easily. As if the other Selkies understood, the pod dispersed. When he peered through gray-green water for their multi-colored pelts, they weren't there.

By the time he clambered onto the rocky shore, Celene had shucked her skin. In human form, she opened her arms to welcome him. Long black hair shrouded her almost to her feet. Violet eyes gleamed in welcome. Her generous breasts peeked through the curtain of hair, their copper-colored nipples already pebbled with wanting him.

Angus had tucked his clothes beneath a rock before joining the Selkie pod. Because he swam nude, nothing was in the way as he plunged into Celene's offered embrace. God, how he'd missed the touch of another against him, skin to skin. Celene's body felt warm against his chilled one. She closed her arms around him and ran her hands down his back, lingering over the curve of his butt.

He hugged her in return. The scent of her, salt and mint, flooded his mind with images of their lovemaking, and his cock hardened between their bodies. He trailed his fingertips down her smooth skin, marveling at how different she felt from a human woman. Velvety and charged with electricity. Some Selkies walked among humans, even took permanent partners. Angus didn't understand how they eluded discovery.

Celene closed her mouth over the junction between his neck and shoulder, licking, sucking, biting. He moved a hand from her back to cup the side of her face and lowered his lips over hers. Desire engulfed him. Hot, urgent, desperate, he sank his tongue into her waiting mouth.

She grappled with his ass, pulling his body hard against hers as her hips writhed and breath hitched in her throat. Tearing her mouth from his, she gasped. "Too long. It's been too long."

Liquid heat trailed the path of her mouth as she licked her way down his chest, stopping to tease his nipples. He kissed the top of her head and wove his fingers into her long hair. Every nerve came alive with wanting her, but it ran deeper than that. Touch was such a basic need, and he'd denied that essential part of his humanity—along with every other comfort.

For what?

No matter how much he gave the Celts, they took every shred—and him—for granted. He wanted to get a job, blend in with humans. Something mundane like driving a cab, or flipping burgers in a grill, but his requests were denied. The Celts provided for him. So long as they housed and fed him, why would he need to clutter his time with anything as humdrum as earning a living? What if they needed him, and he was in the middle of washing dishes in some nameless restaurant? He could almost hear Gwydion's voice. See the master enchanter with a long-suffering look on his face—

He wiped his Celtic masters from his mind. This time was for him and Celene. No one else belonged in his head. Just because he'd chosen a semimonastic existence was no reason he couldn't give her everything she needed. Months had passed since they'd last been together, maybe as much as a year. He moved back enough to fill his hands with her breasts, rubbing her erect nipples before he bent to suck on them, remembering the little biting motions she loved.

A low, guttural moan escaped her, and she threaded her fingers through his hair. Holding him against her breasts, she began to sing as he loved her. A series of low, sweet notes rose in cadence and intensity as she lost herself in his touch. He'd asked her about the music once, and she told him it was how sea people vocalized their joy. The music filled him with unbearable hunger—poignant, mind-bending need for another person's touch.

Although he'd never done it before, he raised his voice and joined her song. The change was instantaneous. In that moment, he sensed her loneliness and isolation, twin to his own and recognized that both of them needed more kisses, more touches—even more than they needed sex.

"Lay on your belly." His voice rasped with wanting her. He tore tufts of marsh grass and arranged them to make her a bed on a sandy stretch between rocks.

She lay down, continuing to sing. Angus sang too, as he straddled her and ran his hands down her back rubbing tension from her muscles. He followed his hands with his mouth and strung kisses across her shoulder blades and down the line of vertebrae from her neck to the curves of her ass. Between their song, the feel of her skin beneath his fingertips, and his cock getting stiffer by the moment, waiting became almost painful, yet he held back, not quite sure why.

The rhythm and cadence of her song shifted as he alternated his mouth and hands across the sculpted planes of her back. The intense pressure in his balls receded almost as if he'd reached a peak, though he hadn't come. Maybe she sensed his need for warmth, contact, much as he'd sensed hers.

"Move off me so I can look at you." Celene flipped over to face him, kneeling above her. Rose and gold splotched her pale skin, and a broad smile split her exotic, high-cheek-boned face. "Today was different. You sang with me. You've never done that before."

He shrugged, suddenly self-conscious. "It felt right. Even though I wasn't inside you, what happened between us felt right."

She cocked her head to one side and trained her gaze on him. "Are you sure you don't have sea blood?"

A flicker of annoyance at the Celts' staunch refusal to disclose anything about his birth narrowed his eyes. "I have no idea what I am." He ticked what he did know off on his fingers. "I'm not immortal, but I'll live well beyond human lifespans. My magic is closer to seer and witch than anything else, yet I'm neither of those. The covens acknowledge me as one of theirs, but only because the local witches are too kind to tell me to go away. The time-travel portals accept me." He shrugged again. "I don't suppose knowing more would make a hell of a lot of difference."

"You're not from Scotland, even though you live there." She stated it baldly, as fact.

He frowned. "Why would you say that?"

"Your speech. There's something about the lilt of Scotland that's impossible to rid yourself of. You don't sound Irish or British, either, at least not from the time we live in." Her nostrils flared. "Maybe that's it."

"Maybe what's it?"

"You could be from the past, and not just a few years back, perhaps hundreds—or even more. I'm not old enough to recall what human speech sounded like then, but some Selkies are."

"Fine." Frustration tightened his chest, like it always did when the mystery of his origins became a point of discussion. "My first memories are when the god of the dead dragged me out of a time-travel portal when I was fifteen."

"I'm sorry." She draped a hand over his hip, cradling it. "I've upset you."

He started to protest, but she silenced him with a look. "Don't insult me with a lie, Angus, but you don't have to talk about it, either. Such a pretty man." She stroked hair back from his face. "With your deep brown hair and amber eyes. Did you know they shade to dark gold when you're angry?"

She was trying to divert him with flattery, but he wasn't buying it. "You have no idea what it's like not knowing—" He shook his head, and the rest of his words died unspoken. It didn't matter what she knew or didn't know about him. She'd never be more than an occasional lover, and both of them knew it.

"It could be more," she said softly, obviously having been in his mind.

Angus took her hands in his and gazed at her. "You get more of me than anyone, and you see how pathetically little that is. There's nothing more to give."

"There could be," she persisted. "You could refuse next time they send you on—"

He bent toward her and laid a hand over her mouth. "I'm not free. Not now. Not ever."

"I don't understand." She pushed his hand away and closed very white teeth over her full lower lip.

He smiled crookedly. "Not sure I do, either. Every man has a life's work. No matter how I feel about it, this appears to be mine."

Even though it wasn't wise, he started to ask what she knew about his current assignment, but a flash of unusual energy drew his gaze skyward. He leapt to his feet. A copper-colored dragon circled to land not far from him. Maybe the Ancient One had seen him with Celene and decided to be considerate.

Not very fucking likely. Dragons were a force unto themselves.

"I have to go," he said. "Let me walk you to your skin, so I know you're safely on your way home."

A sad expression crossed her face, creasing the skin around her eyes into a network of fine lines. "It's right here." She scrambled to her feet and gripped both his upper arms, forcing him to look at her. "Thank you."

"For what?"

"Being you." She brushed her lips over his and moved to a marsh grass thicket. In moments, she'd dragged her pelt over her human body. Transformed into a seal, she waded into the surf.

Before it engulfed her, she turned to gaze at him. *"Be careful, and think on what I said."*

He didn't answer, just watched her head bob in the waves before turning toward his clothing. It wasn't far from the place Celene had led them. His body felt vibrant, alive, and he still tingled from her touch. He longed for a woman of his own, children, a home, before he stuffed the impossible so deep under wraps he couldn't mourn the loss.

Angus moved the large rock he'd placed over his clothes to protect them from the wind. He pulled a ragged dark blue fisherman's knit sweater over his head and stepped into thick, black woolen trousers. Settling on a log, he pulled on socks and laced up stout leather boots. Though the breeze was raw, he'd worn neither hat nor gloves.

Ready as he figured he'd ever be, he covered the fifty yards to where the dragon had settled up the beach. He didn't recognize this one, but he'd only met a bare handful of the hundreds living in Fire Mountain and on other worlds as well. When he drew near, he stopped and bowed his head respectfully, waiting for the dragon to speak first.

"I don't like this any better than you do," the dragon muttered. "Come close enough I don't have to broadcast our business to the world."

Angus walked closer. He could've suggested the dragon use telepathy since all the Ancient Ones were conversant in the technique, but he kept his mouth shut. The dragon was smaller than many he'd seen. Copper scales shaded to burnished gold on its chest, and dark eyes with golden centers whirled so fast they held a hypnotic quality. Lethal, six-inch-long red claws tipped its stubby forelegs. The dragon stood upright on hind legs tipped with the same sharp claws and kept its gaze averted, not saying anything.

What the hell? Every other dragon he'd met was proud, imperious, and quick to remind Angus of his inferiority. This one seemed young, but was it? After another long few minutes, Angus tossed respect—and caution—to the winds.

"What's your name? And what are we supposed to be doing? All Ceridwen told me was to meet you here."

The dragon opened its mouth, and a gout of flame landed scant inches from Angus's boots.

He frowned and drew his brows together. "If we're going to work together, I need to know what to call you." He sent a speculative gaze across the air between them. "If you annihilate me, they'll just assign you a new partner, and I'm a hell of a lot easier to get along with than any of the Celts."

"Tell me something I don't know," the dragon rumbled and belched smoke.

Frustration in its voice struck a note in Angus's soul, and he gestured with both hands. "You may as well tell me who you are and what we're supposed to do together." He infused his words with subtle persuasion. If the dragon didn't care for the Celts, either, they'd likely get along well enough.

"Why? What I should do is leave." The dragon sounded sulky—and scared.

"If you could, you'd already be gone." Angus was as certain of that as he was of anything. The dragon needed him for something, and whatever it was, the Ancient One wasn't particularly proud of it. "What happened? Am I some sort of punishment for you?" Tension settled like a steel bar across his shoulders, and he curled his hands into fists before he realized what he'd done.

"Oh I'd be gone, would I?"

The dragon ignored Angus's questions, and it mimicked his tone with eerie precision. It furled its wings and flapped them a time or two. Dirt swirled; small pebbles slapped Angus in the face. The creature belched steam and looked so distraught, he felt sorry for it.

"My life's not exactly a picnic, either," he ventured, on a hunt for common ground. "I'm a permanent mercenary, with no time off and no possibility of parole."

That got the dragon's attention, and it focused its whirling gaze on him. The golden centers of its eyes deepened with fiery motes that looked like little shooting stars. "Why would you want a respite from being a warrior?"

Good question.

"Because I'm tired. I'd like what most men have."

"What's that?" The dragon raised its brows, and its scales clanked against each other in a dissonant tinkling.

He shook his head. "It doesn't matter. The sooner you spit out whatever you need to say, the easier it'll be. The worst part about holding something you're ashamed of inside is it eats at you until you're nothing but a hollow shell."

Wings flapped, and those intense, whirling eyes shifted to the rocky beach. "I'm not *ashamed* of anything. I've been banished. Ceridwen said if I worked with you—and we were successful—I might be able to return."

Angus kept surprise out of his voice. "Banished from Fire Mountain?"

Steam puffed from the dragon's open mouth. "No. Idiot. I could live with that. They've banished me from the Highlands. My home."

"What happened?"

"It doesn't matter." The dragon threw his words back at him. "We have to go to Fire Mountain, where I'm to find one of the First Born. Once we have him—or her—"

"One of the six First Born dragons?" Angus broke in, scarcely believing the dragon's words. "They'll never show themselves—unless it's in their best interest."

Another wing flap and a defiant head toss. "There are actually ten. One of them was my father."

"When's the last time you saw him?" The words slipped out before he could stop them. Dragon males frequently didn't hang about once mating was over with, but the trembling mass of scales in front of him likely didn't need to be reminded.

"Never. Mother said he was too immersed in battles on another world to return for our hatching."

Angus unclenched his fists and hunted for something soothing to say that wasn't an outright lie. Dragon energy poked past his wards and into his mind. He tried to block it, but couldn't.

"You believe locating a First Born is hopeless." The dragon sounded resigned. "I may as well throw myself into a crater at Fire Mountain. I'll never see the Highlands again—or my mate." More wing rustling and the dragon rose a few feet off the ground, clearly intent on leaving.

"Hold on." Angus loped forward until he was right beneath the dragon. "I didn't say that—or think it, either. I don't know enough to make any sort of judgment. How about if you start at the beginning? If we're going to work together, I deserve that much."

The dragon circled a few times, indecision stamped in its erratic flight pattern.

"I know what it is to be alone." He kept his voice gentle. "And to not have anyone who cares if I live or die."

Maybe it wasn't totally true. Celene might shed a tear or two, but she'd be the only one. He kept his gaze trained on the sky, relieved the dragon wasn't putting distance between them. Something about the creature's pain tugged at his heart and made it feel like a kindred spirit.

The copper dragon folded its wings and settled heavily to earth a few feet from where Angus stood. It straightened its shoulders and tipped its chin defiantly.

"My name is Eletea," the dragon announced, revealing its gender.

"Angus Shea, though you likely know that."

"Yes, I do. I killed a mage, who fancied herself a dragon shifter." Eletea's eyes whirled faster, as if she dared Angus to say something.

He crinkled his forehead as he dredged up what he knew about dragon shifters. "Don't mages take their chances when they show up seeking a dragon to pair with?"

She nodded once, sharply. "The mage seduced one of us into believing her. I saved him by killing her, but he turned on me. Reported me to the Dragons' Council, and they roped the Celts into deciding my fate, since the one I killed had Celtic blood." Eletea's scales rippled in the dragon equivalent of a shrug. "I don't understand why they're bothering. It's not like I went after one of the gods. They're immortal. The one all the fuss is over barely qualified as a Celt."

Angus kept his expression neutral. "Celtic blood aside, I thought mages only bonded with same sex dragons."

"That was another problem," Eletea said, sounding vindicated. "No one saw it but me, though."

Sensing the worst was out on the table, Angus settled on a nearby rock and invited, "Start at the beginning. We have time."

"No, we don't," Eletea protested. "We should've been at Fire Mountain yesterday." She hung her head. "I didn't know what I wanted to do, so I flew and flew and flew. I almost didn't land this afternoon."

Angus did his best to project optimism. "Let's open a time-travel portal and be on our way to Fire Mountain." At the dragon's reluctant nod, he went on. "I understand you have your own ways of returning home, but if you travel with me, you can fill me in as we go."

What he didn't say was it probably wouldn't matter when they arrived at the dragons' home world. First Borns wouldn't give them the time of day, whether they showed up early, late, or right on time. He held many concerns, such as what would a First Born do, assuming they could locate one? But he held those cares inside for now.

He could've dreamed the future. Instead, he summoned a spell to take them to a time-traveling portal. Once the undulating gray-pink tube admitted them, he gradually paid out questions.

Reticent and quiet at first, Eletea finally began to talk.